Accidental Rebels

BLUE FEATHER BOOKS, LTD.

This book is dedicated to the memory of my mother, Ann Sinclair, who from day one was my champion, and to my late partner, Nita McCuller, who pushed me to reach for my dreams.

Accidental Rebels

A BLUE FEATHER BOOK

by
Kelly Sinclair

NOTE: If you purchased this book without a cover, you should be aware that it is stolen property. It was reported as "unsold and destroyed" to the publisher, and neither the author nor the publisher has received any payment for this "stripped book."

This is a work of fiction. All characters, locales and events are either products of the author's imagination or are used fictitiously.

ACCIDENTAL REBELS

Copyright © 2009 by Kelly Sinclair

All rights reserved. No part of this book may be reproduced in any manner whatsoever without written permission from the publisher, save for brief quotations used in critical articles or reviews.

Cover design by Ann Phillips

A Blue Feather Book
Published by Blue Feather Books, Ltd.

www.bluefeatherbooks.com

ISBN: 978-0-9794120-5-9

First edition: January, 2009

Printed in the United States of America and in the United Kingdom.

Acknowledgements

Thanks to Jane Vollbrecht for her editorial wisdom, to my readers over the years, and to members of the Rainbow Leisure Lodge—the ladies who lunch.

Chapter 1

July 1989

"I bet you I can name every faggot in this town."

Hilario Aldaiz guided his '62 Ford pickup over the thin strip of gravel leading to Jackie's Place. A quarter inch of rain the night before, known by local standards as a gullywasher, had been so quickly absorbed into the land that the afternoon sun revealed only a few puddles, hardly enough to coat a tire, much less create a road hazard.

Mandy Gabriel thought it over. No gay living in Tantona who had half a brain would ever come out, not if they wanted to avoid getting fired, or maybe even being arrested. Everyone knew that sodomy was both a sin and a crime.

What was that phrase that writer used? "Only connect." E.M. Forster. Mandy came across his book at the library. She'd like to see Forster try to connect with anyone surviving undercover in Tantona. For that matter, Mandy had yet to drive into nearby Lubbock and check out its gay bar.

Only connect? Impossible. *Every gay here is in hiding, and probably alone, just like me.*

Hilario looked at her impatiently. Okay, there was the drama teacher at Tantona High School, who, despite the wife and two little girls, acted effeminate. There was Hilario himself, who toiled as a cook at El Flaco, his family's restaurant.

"Men only?"

The pickup rolled to a halt in the alley behind a tin-roofed hut. Hilario leaned back in his seat, scornful.

"Don't try and make it easy, girlfriend. I said I could name them all."

They were both dressed in shorts and T-shirts, but there the resemblance ended, as Mandy's top vowed allegiance to Texas Tech and Hilario's to Texas A&M, schools whose doors they had darkened, if little else, in a combined three years.

Mandy knew Hilario back in high school, but even though they were both pariahs, he a suspected homosexual and she the daughter of a jailbird, they never reached out to one another from their separate hells.

Currently neighbors in the South Pecan Street government-housing complex, they shared secrets and drinks on their back porches. An accumulation of such moments made them friends, or people lacking alternatives. Mandy didn't know which, but anyone needing to kill time on a Saturday could do worse than to call up Hilario.

Jackie's Place was supposed to have sinfully delicious barbecue, but Mandy had never driven to the Flatville neighborhood for a brisket sandwich. Wiley, Jackie's oldest son, poked his head out the back door. Seeing familiar faces, he stepped out onto the porch.

"What can I do you for?"

"Four tallboys and three pins." Hilario fanned the dollars in his hand.

"Make that four pins," Mandy said.

Wiley went back inside.

Anyone looking for unopened cans of beer ought to be trying someplace other than a small Texas town that segregated its drinkers into private clubs. *Private. What a joke.* Anyone could join for three bucks. Those feeling too thirsty for the drive to the Lubbock Strip chose Jackie's Place, which the police shut down on average about once a year. Jackie would then splash the hut with fresh paint and reopen after she finished paying off her fine for operating a drive-through.

In Mandy's next article about illicit behavior for the *Tantona Tribune*, she could make it first person; that is, if she wanted to file for unemployment benefits. Folks would probably rather read about a doctor in town rumored to be a cokehead. Her boss, a watered-down vanilla shake of a man, talked about the rumor on late press nights but expressed no interest in investigating.

She decided to address Hilario's topic of the day. "I know about Barbara Wolfe and her lady friend."

Barbara ran Wolfe Auto Parts ever since the death of her father. The lady friend, Darlene something, worked in a lawyer's office on the downtown square.

Mandy once saw them in church for the annual Christmas cantata. They sat by themselves. Some of the members talked to Darlene, but Barbara broadcast such a fierce attitude, not many wanted to risk getting singed. They were pretty old, maybe in their early fifties. Slim and auburn-haired, Darlene looked in better shape than her rougher-edged partner. Barbara had gone through hard times, according to Mandy's mother who saw her sometimes when she was helping Daddy at the magneto shop.

"Barbara and Darlene? I've seen them at the clubs in Lubbock. They live together in the same house. They ain't even trying to hide it. No, I can name every single faggot in Tantona."

"There's fourteen thousand people living here, and you know all five gays. Big nothing."

A pool of dust stirred by their arrival drifted past her open window, wafting a potent blend of cottonseed, oil drippings, and molasses into the cab.

Wiley came to Mandy's side of the pickup and handed her a paper sack. He frowned at the money she placed on his palm.

"We've gone up a dollar on the pins."

Hilario grabbed the bag and looked inside. "Yeah, but they're pins. Not even trying to be joints."

Mandy didn't like it when Hilario went into his Miss Attitude routine, complete with hand gestures. It didn't go with his muscular build.

"Don't get all high-handed on me, Hillie. It's good smoke," Wiley said.

Mandy pulled out four ones from her wallet to make up the difference.

"You're a sweetie." Wiley liked to flirt with her, despite his lack of success.

Mandy had no illusion that men ogled her because she was a Playboy beauty. The main draws consisted of her mane of Cadillac-black hair and the fact that God gifted her with cleavage, albeit with a height only a gymnast would envy.

Hilario politicked for a trip to Lubbock as they rolled out of Flatville.

"If you were planning on picking up beer at the Strip, we didn't need to go to the boot here," Mandy said.

She had in mind a visit to the King's Pub in Tantona to see bartender Erma Delgado. Erma's feathered hair and dark eyes aided a resemblance to Rosanne Cash, and her smile did seem to linger in

Mandy's direction. A touch more nerve or maybe another tallboy and she might ask Erma to Hilario's birthday party next weekend.

"Hell yeah, we do. We need to get ourselves in the mood."

"What about the King's?"

"Forget about Erma. She has a boyfriend. Mickey Reyes. He's a real man."

Hilario's ideal of masculinity involved the holy trinity of vehicle, chest hair, and income, with the example varying from week to week, depending on whether the real man ticked off Hilario or some member of his family.

He tunelessly sang along to "Candy" by Cameo on his cassette player. Hilario stopped mid-line. "And I sure as hell know who's gay. You ain't been there at the glory hole Saturday nights. All those Tantona faggots driving to Lubbock for some head."

"Wouldn't you just see the, you know, the part and not the face?"

She took a hit off a joint as they came to a stop on a gravel road behind the well-kept Mexican cemetery. She had always viewed pot as half-high, half-medicine, depending on how hard her period cramps were hitting, but lately it served as a tranquilizer, getting her through that long stretch of empty known as her weekend.

Momma kept asking her to come back to church, as if that was a solution. What, and sit there meek and mild as she was being condemned to everlasting hellfire? She already knew where she was headed. Momma ought to be satisfied with Daddy's attendance, given that Mandy's three brothers were confirmed backsliders.

"Tantona faggots." Hilario refused to let his topic die. "I see them in the dirty bookstore, and I see their cars in the parking lot, like when you see the boozers at the Strip in Lubbock. They can roll up looking nice, pretending they're not from here. They ain't so pretty 'long about two in the morning. Me, I'm pretty anytime."

He worked the youthful look, plucking gray hairs whenever he spotted them, even though he was about to match Mandy's age of twenty-eight. She figured he would pluck his head bald at the rate he was going.

The mixtape moved on to Karyn White's "Superwoman." The two said little until they worked down the beers and a couple of joints.

"You want to come watch MTV with me?" Mandy said.

"Nah, I gotta call my man."

That would be Hilario's mystery maybe-lover, Tommy somebody. She had been sitting in Hilario's bedroom when he argued on the phone with Tommy about a date that fell through. The relationship seemed real enough; more real than her and Erma, at any rate.

* * *

Every workday, Tina Ransom walked eight blocks from her duplex apartment on Souther Street to the library, a routine easy enough to follow on weekday mornings, but not on a smoldering Saturday afternoon. It didn't speak well for her judgment, but she did make it to the back porch in one piece, however toasted.

She opened the door with her key and went down the hallway to her office, her first breath of cool respite. The exercise helped to clear the fog from her mind. She tucked her purse into a filing cabinet drawer, and after snagging the day's third Coke out of the refrigerator, she sat down at her desk.

"Eh," called out Otilia Garcia, who was one of her part-timers. Otilia covered the few steps from the checkout desk to Tina's office in her usual pumping stride and pulled the door shut behind her.

"That man is here again."

"Who?" Tina thought she might already know the answer.

"McBride."

He visited Tantona twice yearly, setting up shop in the library where he read the newspaper, snuck bites of food from his backpack, and cleaned up in the public bathroom. Mr. McBride ranked low on Tina's list of problem patrons, but Otilia didn't like his crumbs or his attitude.

"He'll be gone in a week or so." Tina applied a soothing tone to her words.

"Not soon enough," Otilia said. "You weren't here that time he stole all the paper towels from the men's restroom. You don't know what kind of trouble he can get into."

That was her way of reminding Tina that, at a mere thirteen years of service, she was but a neophyte compared to Otilia, who started at the library two decades ago, back when Tina, a Texas Tech sophomore, was pummeling History of Medieval Europe.

"Mr. McBride hasn't been much trouble lately. I think we can tolerate him for the week or so he's usually here."

"Maybe so," Otilia said. She thrust the door open and returned to the checkout desk.

Tina and her first assistant, Mary Eckert, traded off on Saturday afternoons, except that today, Mary was still on vacation with her husband, a shy pharmacist Mary always referred to by his full name. They were in New York City to see a Sondheim musical and some off-Broadway productions. Mary's current project, one of many plates she kept aloft, involved resuscitating the local theatre group, which collapsed after last year's flop with *The Cherry Orchard*.

"Chekhov isn't a good fit for our town," Mary said to her at the time. "He's too dry."

"This is a dry town, in more ways than one, and maybe you were too ambitious."

"I might be inclined to agree with you, but *The Glass Menagerie* was huge for us, and so was *Bus Stop*. Barlow Eckert says folks like a little juice in their apple."

When Mary returned, she would be laden with playbills and tales of near-muggings and authentic bagels, but what would Tina have to offer by comparison? Her week wound down with the usual book orders, the usual overdues by the usual patrons, and if there had been a moment the whole time that wasn't ordinary, she didn't know about it.

Wouldn't a trip to New York be pure bliss, even if paying for it would cut into her savings? She looked up when the front doorbell tinkled. Sydney Melston came in with a load of what had to be books for donation.

Tina looked up to Sydney, literally, who topped out a good six feet by Tina's reckoning. Sydney had wavy blonde hair threaded with gray, and hazel eyes that appeared startled no matter the occasion. She showed up from time to time with boxes from the personal library of her mother, who, after having nursed her husband to a not-early-enough demise from Alzheimer's disease, dropped dead of a heart attack over a year ago. Sydney taught high school English, but Tina didn't remember much about her from her teaching days. Perhaps they both tended toward shyness back then.

More than once, Tina considered suggesting to Sydney that she come over and help sort through the books. That would be a kind thing to do, and so what if it was a selfish move on her part? She was sure Syd had no idea what thoughts idled in Tina's head.

She caught up to Sydney by the magazine rack and asked about her melon patch.

"I started late on planting, but I'm beginning to see a few baby melons. Tiny little things, but they have to start somewhere, don't they?" Sydney whisked an *Atlantic Monthly* magazine into her arms.

"I'd be glad to come over sometime and go through the books with you," Tina said before she could stop herself.

"That would be great. Would you? I don't want to hang on to everything, but I don't know what should go to her church and what should go to the library. What's a good night for you to come over?"

"Next Friday, unless you're free that Saturday."

"I'm open next Saturday. I mean, yes, I'm a social reject, no plans whatsoever." Sydney let out a self-deprecating laugh.

"So am I. That is, you're not, but I'm free that night." Sydney's eyes, however alarmed, were riveting.

After firming up their plans, they moved in opposite directions, Sydney heading for the checkout desk and Tina for Mr. McBride. She saw no need for anything more than an "I know you're back in town, and let's agree to be civilized" subtext, which would satisfy Otilia and yet grant Tina an untroubled afternoon.

Mr. McBride alternated his time between Pennsylvania and Southern California. Texas amounted to nothing more than a large obstacle in his life, yet Tantona, "blessed with a shady park and cursed with being in the middle of bumfuck nowhere"—a direct quote from the man—made for a tolerable midsummer fit.

"Damned if I know why it always works out this way," he said. His bushy white eyebrows all but hid his eyes. He looked up from the pages of the *Lubbock Avalanche-Journal*. "I try to get through here before it's too blazing hot, but I can't hardly manage it. Then, here I am, foundering in the wreckage. What happened to the *New York Times*?"

"The lady who paid for our subscription passed away. Have you considered the *Washington Post*?"

Mr. McBride snorted. "Bunch of quiche-eating socialists. They think they're sitting up with Jesus 'cause they broke Watergate. Hell, my brother coulda broke it, and he's not even registered."

Registered as what, a voter? Tina decided not to ask Mr. McBride to clarify his statement. There were more pleasantries, and then she went to the checkout desk to give Otilia a break. *Yes, I've visited with the man; now I can think about Sydney.*

What did she think about Sydney? The birth date on her library card made her forty-seven. She had never been married, but now and then Sydney's name came up in connection with a farmer named Tommy who lived south of town. It didn't sound like an intense relationship, according to Becca Reyes, Tina's duplex neighbor and a math teacher at Tantona High School.

"They're more friends than anything," Becca said during one of their Sunday morning jaunts through the neighborhood. "Why? You interested in Tommy?"

Maybe there was no point in reviewing Sydney's maybe's, but it had been over two years since Tina broke off her romance with Sherron Steinhall. Or rather, their affair, which took place over the course of several furtive afternoon visits to Tina's apartment. Sherron came by on weekends when her anesthetist husband was on call at the hospital.

The word romance definitely didn't apply, although Sherron pursued her long enough. It started at the library board's pledge drive kickoff party when Sherron made a remark about being too sexually adventurous for Tantona. Sherron played up that angle during one-on-one moments, until one Sunday afternoon she came up to Tina on the United Supermarket parking lot and extracted an invitation to come over for coffee.

Perhaps that was the first time Sherron had come on to another woman, but she did seem experienced, to put it politely. Sherron struck her as the kind of person who would never leave her family or her affluent lifestyle, who would never cause complications for Tina.

During her first year of college, Tina slept with a couple of different girls, but left all experimentation behind when she came back home. If she ever discussed intimate matters with Mary Eckert, which would be never, she'd ask what made her vulnerable to Sherron. Was her need so obvious, her hunger that plain?

Any revelations made to Mary, however, would end up in Barlow Eckert's ears, and from there to the county judge, her boss. Long ago Tina decided that if the question ever came up, she'd admit to being a sexual criminal in the state of Texas and endure the consequences. Gossip, however, was something she would walk through a field of tumbleweeds to avoid, given what happened with her family. She would do anything to avoid a repeat of all those pitying eyes and speculative remarks.

Sydney wanted her to come over. Probably nothing would come of it, but why not allow the possibility, the bare whisper of something?

* * *

Caterina Talamantez Acuff struggled to understand the client in her husband's chair, who produced sonic bursts of Spanglish with every snip Neil delivered.

In the years since their move to Tantona, Cat continued to make an effort to pick up what was supposed to be her native tongue, but Neil had her beat—Neil, a freckled, bottle-blond with an array of bawdy jokes he picked up from clients. Cat's father didn't consider being bilingual an upwardly mobile skill in Amarillo, so what little Spanish she learned, Mama slipped in via recipes and lullabies. Cat did learn to make tortillas, which Mama believed to be an essential skill for a housewife.

Neil's fluency came from working with the hired hands on his parents' north county farm. He loved all of it: spraying weeds with Roundup, running the sandfighter, and moving sprinkler systems. But after a semester of ag courses at Texas Tech, he moved on to cutting hair in Amarillo. Later, he came to Tantona with a new bride in tow and opened up a salon.

Cat knew people wondered how on earth Neil managed to get her pregnant, especially back in the early days, when he still wore his hair long and had a tiny diamond stud in one earlobe. Bikers and redneck Willies might let their freak flag fly, but not with hair so meticulously layered and streaked. The word got around that, while the Acuff boy might not be the toughest tool in the shed, he had an extremely pregnant young wife, and didn't he have a way with scissors?

Cat turned the music back up and focused on her bookkeeping. "Bastards of Young" by the Replacements was finishing up.

"Who's that?" asked the client who was in the chair in Sandra's stall, her chubby face topped with a patchwork quilt of rollers.

Sandra clipped another roller into place. "Honey, you know it's that crazy music Cat's always listening to. I don't know where you find that stuff. It ain't on the radio."

"If it's not on KLLL, it might as well be from Mars as far as you're concerned," Neil said as he swept his station.

One more remark about the mixtape and Cat might start doing the books at home, although she preferred the percolating atmosphere of Neil's salon.

Sandra managed to ruin the opening line of the next song, "The Wasteland" by the Mission UK. "What did he say?"

"He said that he still believes in God, but God no longer believes in him," Neil answered before Cat had a chance to say anything.

Even Neil has the mixtape memorized now, Cat thought, and this is a man who thinks rock and roll stopped along about the time the Rolling Stones released "Angie."

"Well, that's just plain crazy talk." Sandra shuffled her client over to the dryer. "You should listen to songs that lift you up, give you a reason to get up in the morning, not some weirdo with a funny accent messing with your head."

Cat couldn't stop herself. "Songs like this make me feel I'm seeing how things really are, but if it bothers you, I don't mind turning it off."

"It's y'all's shop, do what you want. I'd like to hear something happy now and then."

Sandra, whose hair stuck out from her head like fried platinum, needed to take her own advice on following a sensible perm schedule.

Vonn Hendricks, a skinny man barely supporting his ginger afro, came in the door carrying his guitar case. He was early for a change, not that Cat minded. She needed more time to work with Vonn, who knew so much about music, about touring, about everything over which she pleaded complete ignorance.

Cat had a decent, although raspy, singing voice. It never worked with the country songs she sang for a time with a local band. Country ruled the clubs, country was all people wanted to hear. Then a few months ago, her son Wesley's best friend's brother left behind some tapes when he moved to central Texas.

Wesley tossed the cassettes onto his desk, but Cat had to hear them again and again until her platonically devoted husband paid a visit to Ralph's Records in Lubbock. He bought an armful of records the frazzle-bearded clerk recommended.

Some of her friends had heard of the Eurythmics and the Pretenders but not Bauhaus, the Jam, the Cure, the Smiths, Jesus and Mary Chain, the Mission UK, and Joy Division. They were mysterious beings living in an England unknown to the Queen and Dusty Springfield.

In her thirty-third year, Cat discovered the beats for which her voice was created. Over the past six months, she rounded up local musicians and had begun working up some songs, trying to balance the band with her bookkeeping, visits to the library, and ferrying Wesley to his school activities. Becca Reyes, one of Neil and Cat's favorite clients, showed up one time in the back room of the shop, where the band practiced evenings and weekends, and proclaimed them the new Stones.

Their music came out less British and more garage band, which was why, lately, she paid more attention to the Replacements, an American group. They managed to sound good while sucking at the same time.

Cat caught a glimpse of herself in the floor-length wall mirror. There she was, sitting at a table by the cashier's desk, a copper-skinned, thirty-something woman, wearing too much mascara for a Saturday afternoon.

Her long legs made her look tall until people stood up next to her and realized she was, in reality, of average height. She felt average in a lot of ways, but something happened when she sang. Even Neil remarked on the transformation, saying that she sounded like she had a million miles of restless in her heart. Whatever that meant. Neil tended to let his mouth do the thinking for him.

In Amarillo, she'd been the dutiful daughter of a high-powered car dealer, while in Tantona, people knew her as a responsible wife and mother.

She didn't know how many miles of restless she had, but she did feel something come over her when she sang, something so powerful that it spilled over the edges into her everyday life. Despite her foreign books and videos, those fluent images of other people's lives, she didn't know what to call what was going on. Maybe the more she sang, the closer she'd come to finding out.

She looked up from her ledger to see the drummer walk in the door. Who knew how far she might go today?

Chapter 2

"I'm going to tell you right now, the master bathroom has an old, old shower, but it works. I just two weeks ago took the house off the hands of a lady whose son... The details don't matter, but the house came up available." Mary Eckert whisked Hilario and Mandy to the offending region.

Thank or blame Hilario, who unlike Mandy, actually read the *Tantona Tribune*'s classifieds. Since Mrs. Eckert's first renter's check bounced, they were being rushed through a tour of the three-bedroom, one-and-a-half bath, stucco dump. The house stood on the edge of the Flatville neighborhood, but technically was in Tantona proper, a distinction some white folks might still appreciate, but Mandy didn't care.

She saw concrete walls, touches of mold, and dim lighting seeping in from a small, clouded window by the toilet. It would be like showering in a tomb, not that she had any knowledge of mummy hygiene.

"I have the paint in the garage, but there's no brushes or sheets, none of that. If y'all paint the house inside-out, then all I'd want is first month's rent for you to move in."

Mrs. Eckert led them down the hall, with its faded orange shag carpet and water stains on the ceiling, and through the utility room into a wooden-fenced backyard.

At that point, Hilario, who had been unusually quiet, spoke up. "I know how much total paint goes for, 'cause my uncle does a lot of remodeling. You need to knock off another hundred to make it come out right."

Mrs. Eckert raised her eyebrows in polite disbelief. She didn't look that old, Mandy thought. She'd even look kind of hot if she colored her silver hair and went cold turkey on the tanning habit.

Mandy had seen her earlier in the day when she dropped off a Stephen King novel. Mrs. Eckert was a stickler on getting books back on time, but other than that, nice enough and lively, unlike her boss, Miss Ransom. Mandy thought of that woman as Miss Brown, which described her hair, her clothes, and her dull personality.

"Mr. Aldaiz, I'm not asking for perfection here. All I need is some paint on the walls."

"Lady, I worked for my uncle all through high school and still do sometimes. I'll get it done, I'll get it done right, and I got my own equipment."

Mrs. Eckert studied the two for a moment, then glanced at her watch.

"Tell you what, I need to get home. Barlow Eckert and I are going to Lubbock to eat out, see some friends, and then go watch my son play in a band. Do y'all like unusual music? It's not the Beatles, I'll tell you that much. Jim says they're playing the Rattletrap Club starting at nine. They might appreciate having an audience. Mandy, Mr. Aldaiz, I have an instinct for people, and it's telling me you'll stand by your word. Give me two hundred, and we'll call it square."

Mrs. Eckert left with their checks stuffed in her backpack-sized purse. Mandy and Hilario sat on the concrete front porch, which had a rusted aluminum overhang. The floor felt cool next to her thighs.

"I can't believe we're doing this," she said.

"We talked about it before. What's not to believe, that a place came up we can afford?"

Hilario pulled out a pack of cigarettes. From what he said, his boyfriend, whoever he was, could drive anyone to bad habits. Hilario had so far tested negative for HIV, but who knew whether his mystery boyfriend was as careful.

"What? You're ticked about something."

"Why won't you tell me who your boyfriend is? I wouldn't spread it around."

"I would if I could. Girl, you're my *prima*."

"Don't talk Spanish to me. You won't get off that easy."

"I'll give you a clue. He goes to your church."

"It ain't my church, not anymore."

Not since Brother Jesse ratted her out to her parents. Momma, slow in some ways, couldn't understand what being gay was supposed to mean, but Daddy swiftly withdrew Mandy's Sunday dinner plate. The church had been her home since middle school; then Brother Jesse turned it into a wrestling arena where she couldn't possibly compete.

"I thought you liked holy rolling."

"Don't call it that. Anyhow, will he be at the party?"

"No. Maybe. No, I don't think so, and we need to hit the road. Erlinda wants me to bring some ice."

His older sister lived out in the country in a trailer with a big yard. It was perfect for parties, if one didn't mind stepping around her assortment of lawn ornaments. Maybe ornaments was too fancy a word for plastic dolls planted in the soil like so many Disney gnomes, but Mandy didn't know what to call them except weird, although not to Erlinda's face.

The one time Hilario did drag in Lubbock, as preserved in his photograph album, he made a more convincing woman than his sister.

"Ice to your own party? Sister's got you running errands."

"I don't mind. She's cooking." That was all he needed to say.

By the time they worked through Hilario's wardrobe to find his most slimming black shirt, dropped by Mandy's apartment to pick up his present, and stopped to buy bags of ice, they were running late.

Erlinda, not one to allow premature consumption of her brisket, had kept friends and family at bay with bottles of Tecate until her feckless little brother showed up, that *cabrone*, thinking he could make her smile with a goosey *cumbia* step.

Watching Hilario joke with his sister made Mandy wish she and her three brothers got along that well. She never talked to Chuck, Douglas, or Jimmy about the thoughts rattling around in her head, the women she almost asked out, or the woman she dated the summer after she graduated from high school. Once they officially found out, which was over a year ago, they delegated Jimmy, the youngest, to talk to Mandy about the abomination of homosexuality.

Whoever taught Jimmy that phrase couldn't have been from the family Gabriel. It had to have come straight from the mouth of Brother Jesse, a preacher who didn't believe in keeping secrets.

When they were kids, Douglas used Mandy and Jimmy as interchangeable punching dummies, something Daddy did nothing to stop.

"It's a hard world. Y'all need toughening up," he would say, deep into a twelve-pack. Daddy may have left the booze behind, but Douglas and Jimmy saw no reason to adopt more civilized ways. The oldest brother, Chuck, had the sense to escape to Alaska, albeit leaving a pregnant girlfriend behind.

Yet Mandy was considered the shame of the family.

It took two beers and half a joint with Hilario before her anger evaporated into a warm haze. She packed some brisket into one of

Erlinda's sublime tortillas, sat in a deck chair by the wading pool, and managed half a taco until it landed on her Adidas. She won a stare-down with Erlinda's chow chow, who wanted to handle the cleaning, then she headed for the bathroom. The shoelaces would need washing, but after scrubbing, her shoes returned to their normal pristine white.

She started out the back door, only to hear Hilario talking heatedly to Erlinda in the yard. In the background, a Mazz tape blared a spine-thumping bass line.

"Don't do it, Hillie," Erlinda said in her husky voice. "Making you walk down that road—won't even come to your party. Call him back."

"It's too late. He left already." Hilario sounded strained, vulnerable. "I told him I'd be at the Oliver place. He's expecting me. I won't be gone long."

"That *vendejo*. I oughta put a hurtin' on him. And you ain't going alone. It's too dark out there."

"Hell no, you ain't coming with me. He wouldn't stop if he saw you. And I'm not taking the car, 'cause the others would know something's up and try to spy on me."

Mandy stepped out onto the porch. "I'll go."

Erlinda threw up her hands and stumped into the trailer.

"Come on," Hilario said.

By the time they set out, the moon had collapsed into a sliver in the dusty night sky. Cleaving to the middle of the deeply-rutted road, they arrived at a tractor half-buried in sand. That and a run-down shed constituted the old Oliver homestead.

Hilario and Mandy liked shooting off their revolvers in the caliche pit out back, executing plastic milk bottles in a place with no one to complain about the noise. At the moment, she could have used some kind of human sounds. All she could hear was the wind and, out of the west, low keening sounds coming from coyotes or feral dogs in the area.

"You stay back here and don't say nothing. Remember, you didn't see him."

"I can't see my hands, Hillie, let alone anyone else."

Wobbly headlights appeared a quarter mile distant, but closing fast.

"He's gonna break an axle the way he's driving. I tell him to take it easy, but he's gotta be the *macho* with his truck. Always."

"How did you meet him?"

He laughed harshly. "Everybody knows about me. Some of them before I did. Okay, you stay here and be quiet."

A long, dark pickup pulled onto the turnrow leading to the caliche pit. It traveled a few yards before stopping, with Hilario already there to greet his lover. There was a brief flash of light when he got in the passenger side, enough for Mandy to recognize the man.

Tommy Williams sat behind the wheel. Mandy called him sometimes when she needed to quote rainfall amounts from area farmers, and yes, he attended Mandy's former church. He had the blocky build of an aging jock. Moments later, Hilario burst out of the pickup and down the road with Tommy jogging to catch up to him.

"Why are you so mad at me, Hillie? Didn't you like the present?"

Hilario came to a halt. Waving the box around, he railed, "You give me this? Some damned cologne?"

"It's the brand you like, and Dillard's didn't have it on sale, that's for sure. If you don't want it—"

"Screw you, Thomas. I can't sit down at my family's restaurant with you. I can't go to your house during the day. Hell, I can't even talk to you when we happen to be in the store at the same time. You're so afraid somebody will see us and know we're together. You're so weirded out when people, they don't know what's going on. You could say I'm doing odd jobs for you. That's how it's done, but no, you… you don't want to. I'm sick of it."

Hilario turned to tramp back toward Erlinda's place. Mandy watched Tommy return to his pickup and deliver a kick to the passenger-side door that had to leave a sizable dent.

He left the door open, the light creating a halo for his close-cut hair as he leaned his head on the steering wheel. He looked like the loneliest man in the county. It felt strangely intimate to Mandy, watching him from behind the tractor, with sandy loam crunching under her shifting shoes and the breeze carrying smells of barbecue from down the road.

On some night, would she end up being the one in the pickup, trying to make a life out of such threadbare moments, or would she be Hilario? She fumbled around the far side of the tractor, managing not to attract Tommy's attention. A few yards down the road, she ran in the ruts, careless of where she placed her feet in the flooding darkness.

* * *

Tina nibbled on a slice of Gouda, enjoying the view, or the lack thereof, from her host's gazebo. A quartet of cherry trees joined with the ivied trellises in blocking any view from the sides or alley of the gazebo's interior, while the view inside was Italian-restaurant dim.

Tina had managed to log twenty minutes of book-sorting before Sydney—"call me Syd"—took her off to the closet in her guest bedroom to display a collection of movie magazines, which were for the most part lurid 1950s exposés.

In one of them, an actress named Lizabeth Scott stood accused of consorting with strange women. Syd purchased them in a garage sale, thinking they might be valuable. Asked for her opinion, Tina had none, other than thinking to herself that Lizabeth Scott's dating habits might be why she never heard of her. She wondered if Syd was trying to send her a message.

Some mood music, a cheese plate, and a bottle of wine later, she was now parked on a wicker chair in the gazebo. At this rate, Tina would finish weeding through Syd's books in a year of Saturdays, not that she felt any need to complain.

"I bet you thought I fell in." Syd settled into the chair to Tina's right. "I had to take out my contacts. They were starting to bother me." The change to glasses seemed to make her look more relaxed, although given the lighting, Tina couldn't tell for certain.

"There's something I want to talk to you about. It's been on my mind for a while, and I hope it's okay with you." Syd paused.

Tina floundered for a response. Who was about to be outed: Syd or herself? "Go right ahead."

"I've sort of known you for a long time. I know it's none of my business, but I think you're really attractive."

Tina's stomach flip-flopped.

"I never, ever see you in jeans."

"Pardon?"

"You dress too old. Those slacks, for instance—they're okay, I guess, but you need younger clothes." Syd refilled both their glasses. "I see your helpers on Saturdays wearing jeans, but you never do."

"I guess it's because I was fairly young when I took the position, compared to who'd been there before, so I wanted to dress the part." Tina thought of her clothes as protective coloration.

"That was then, this is now. There are places in town that do casual Fridays. You should go in with that. I know you were like me for a long time. You had a lot of illness in your family, so you couldn't get out much. That's why I thought it would be okay to talk to you about it. We have so much in common."

It wasn't a gay moment, then.

"I guess we do," Syd said. "Don't we? Except for me, it was my mother who was ill for a long time."

Tina tried not to show her disappointment that it was family member illnesses, not their own brand of alleged mental illness, that Syd saw as common ground.

"And your brother, Jack. God," Syd added in a rush, "I'm so sorry I brought him up. I guess I thought—"

"He's been gone a long time. I can talk about it."

Mary Eckert sometimes shared anecdotes about pranks Jack used to pull as a teen volunteer. Over time, Tina had developed a tolerance to hearing her stories. Comfort was another matter.

She wished she could only remember her older brother as the jokester and not as someone whose early-onset Huntington's Disease destroyed him in four years, turning a gym rat into a slack-jawed, drooling wreck. She couldn't forget the way his eyes kept darting back and forth as he sat strapped into the wheelchair, watching a Lakers game on their living room television. Maybe he was watching.

Even so, he had it better than Mom, who first started showing symptoms in the year before Jack died of pneumonia. Mom took nine years dying and would have gone longer if Dad hadn't accidentally given her too large a Haldol injection one night after he moved her out of the nursing home.

"I can talk about it." *All in all, I would have preferred a pass from you rather than fashion advice.* "But, getting back to the clothes problem."

"I wouldn't call it a problem."

"It's a problem, because I don't know what's current and what would look good on me."

"Maybe we could go to Lubbock and shop at the Mall."

Before Tina left, they firmed up plans to visit the South Plains Mall Sunday after next. At the door, Syd leaned down and hugged her. "Let's do this again, and soon. I had a good time."

"So did I."

As she opened the screen door, Tina felt Syd's lips brush her cheek. She turned to see Syd, her back turned and heading down the hallway.

It took Tina a moment to find the handle, and it wasn't until she walked through her own front door that she realized she'd neglected to turn off her car lights. After correcting that oversight, she went back inside, noticing on the way that her neighbor Becca Reyes's car was gone.

She and Becca liked hanging out together, whether for watching videos or teaming up for backyard barbecues. Unlike Tina, Becca had a social life that took her to Lubbock on most weekends. *At least someone gets out now and then.* Her fingers touched where Syd's kiss had landed.

Mary Eckert sometimes planted a kiss on Tina's cheek on the occasion of a birthday and meant nothing by it. Something told her that this kiss carried more-complicated freight.

* * *

Even with it being fifteen minutes to showtime, all Cat could think about was spelling.

There were examples of illiteracy on the unisex bathroom wall, not to mention a hand-painted sign near the club entrance that advised customers not to "spite" on the floor.

Wesley almost talked her into letting him ride with them to the show, but she was glad their friends, the Hortons, who treated Wesley as one of their own, included him in their plans to go to the drag races that night. She would rather play for her son on a better-planned occasion.

Most of her lyrics were nakedly personal, which might be hard to explain to her son, much less to her friends. No one in the band, Blue Movie, had ever asked her why a housewife and bookkeeper wrote lines expressing frustration and alienation. Maybe they thought it was nothing but an act, or more likely, they only listened for the chord changes.

"Ready?" Neil closed the door behind him. "What's with the frown? You need to put your game face on. Vonn found his other mike. He wanted you to know."

"Good, because something's wrong with mine. I don't know what."

"He thinks there's a short in your line, but Kentrell has a mike we can borrow."

Cat handed the comb over to him, and Neil went to work, spritzing hairspray in strategic spots.

"I think the entire Carrillo family is here."

Kentrell Dimmells, a high school student, played keyboards, while their rhythm section consisted of bassist Marco Carrillo and drummer Jim Eckert, a lapsed college philosophy major.

"Anyone else?"

"Mary and Barlow Eckert just walked in, along with some women I think might be related to Kentrell." Black, in other words. "It's not a bad turnout when you consider how y'all just got the job day before yesterday."

The scheduled act's lead singer could hardly do a gig from Lubbock County Jail, where traffic tickets and procrastination had landed him, so Blue Movie was hired, courtesy of Jim, whose claim to know club managers turned out to be true in this case.

"Take a look." Neil led her toward the battered mirror.

Between the cracks, she saw a transformed creature. She was dressed in a form-fitting, sleeveless black top with a silver fishnet overlay half off one shoulder, paired with metallic purple slacks stuffed into calf-high black boots. Thanks to Neil, her hair stiffened in the right places. She topped off the look with thickly applied mascara and black-edged lipstick.

"I would not want to meet me in a dark alley. Thanks, babe."

"Glad you like it. There's a gay bar on the corner. I'm going to hand out flyers to people going in."

"Don't miss the start of the show."

"I wouldn't worry if I were you. The way Vonn's going with the sound check, I'd be surprised if you start on time."

Thirty minutes later, Cat was forced to agree with her husband. The band sounded perfectly in tune, Marco turned down his amp to a setting less than ear bleed, and the microphone problem had been solved.

"Vonn?" She tapped him on the arm.

Vonn jumped about a mile. "What?" Dressed in formal tuxedo pants and a vest, he smelled of fear and marijuana.

"We need to start." As she spoke, she saw Neil come in the door with several people, likely pilgrims from the gay bar.

"I can't remember the first song." His guitar pick flew toward Kentrell as he spoke. Kentrell, looking fly in a bright yellow and green ensemble, went hunting for the pick.

Marco came over and tapped Vonn on his chest. "Jim and me, we've got the rhythm covered. 'Trell and Cat, they're pretty enough to make the crowd forget our ugly faces, so all you need to do is play, and I know you can do that."

Becca Reyes and another woman stood by the door. Neil must have called some of his customers, the hipper ones, to see if they would come support his wife. Bless him. They had some semblance of a crowd.

Catching Jim's eye, she cued him to kick off the first number, which was "I Don't Know Anything." Vonn would have to grow a pair or sit this one out.

> You think I should know what I'm doing,
> 'Cause I've been here long enough.
> Some people have life down to a science.
> They practice the art of love.
> I can't live within my dreams.
> There you go, callin' me a rebel,
> But there ain't no more Jimmy Deans
> If I confuse you sometimes
> I'm sorry, but no,
> I don't know anything about love.
> Show me your mercy sometimes,
> Tell me the secret,
> 'Cause I don't know, I don't know, I don't know.

Vonn came to life midway through the first verse, churning out harsh, spastic chords that matched the choked quality of her voice until everyone opened up on the chorus. Surprisingly, Kentrell remembered the lyrics and his harmony at the same time.

> Keep making it up as I go along,
> Get the feeling right, the words all wrong.
> Breaking rules I never knew existed
> In a social register where I'm not listed.
> And if I'm a rebel, it's accidental,
> This leather jacket's a rental…
> There ain't no more Jimmy Deans.

She saw Marco creeping toward his amp during the second verse. She made a theatrical gesture at him that served the message: don't turn up your amp, or I will kill you after the show.

Jim was supposed to do a few bars of kicking the bass drum while she stalked the front of the bandstand, ad-libbing to the crowd, but instead, animated by the fact that they were at last playing live, he layered on some toms with occasional cymbal crashes. Not to be outdone, Kentrell stabbed some triads in the spaces.

> If I confuse you sometimes
> I'm sorry, but no,
> I don't know anything about love.
> Show me your mercy sometimes,
> Tell me the secret,
> 'Cause I don't know, I don't know, I don't know.

It got louder, then still louder, then came the last chorus, and she couldn't help it, she shrieked, "I don't know, I don't know," while some in the crowd danced wildly and others jumped up and down. Maybe that was their idea of dancing. No one stood stock-still except for Neil, who was in front of the bandstand. She couldn't see his expression through the spotlight, but he had to be smiling.

Vonn wasted no time signaling for them to start the next song. She had to sing some more? Drenched in sweat, she'd exhausted all her emotions on the first number—best not to know how her makeup was holding up—yet from somewhere, more energy came. Later, she would learn to pace herself, but for now, give it all to the crowd.

She survived to the first break, almost staggering to their reserved table, where she drained the first of four margaritas the waitress had lined up before her.

"Don't blame me," Neil said. "They asked about your favorites. I didn't know people wanted to buy you a round."

Mary Eckert claimed one of the drinks and took a swallow. "You ought to do a gig at Dillard's Department Store. Might get a whole new wardrobe if you play your cards right."

Over Mary's shoulder, Cat saw Kentrell sneaking sips from his sister Mimi's glass. There was no sign of Vonn and Marco, which meant they were outside smoking a joint.

God, she was thirsty. She took a deep swallow of her second margarita, thankful that it was on the rocks, and then offered a glass to Barlow Eckert, a shy, balding man who had been eyeing the drinks covetously.

"Next time, we're bringing more outfits so you can change between sets," Neil said. He tried to pluck the fishnet into some semblance of order.

"So there's going to be another time?"

"Without a doubt. The owner wants you for next month. I said maybe, if he went up on the cover."

"Since when did you become our manager?" She gently squeezed Neil's arm.

"Ever since I booked you a gig at Risqué."

"Where?" Cat and Mary said together.

"The club on the corner. The manager came in for a bit while you were singing. He was pretty impressed, so I made a deal on the spot."

She had the feeling there was more involved to the conversation, given Neil's powers of persuasion with certain men. Glancing over to the near corner, she saw Becca and her friend having what appeared to be a serious conversation, make that an argument, to judge by their use of hands. A section of plaid entered her vision. When she looked up, she saw a tall woman in western wear displaying a commercial-strength glistening smile.

"I hope you're working on my drink, but I don't mind if you share."

Cat knew she was gap-mouthed, but it took a moment to get her reactions under control. Mary made a studious effort at clearing her throat, which cued Cat that introductions were in order. Neil had a stiff expression on his face.

"Mary, Barlow, I'd like you to meet Daniela Polchek, an old classmate of mine from Amarillo."

Dani. She had been singing for the past hour in front of Dani, who was both her first and her last lover. Vonn thought he had a case of nerves. Now Cat would have to go back up there and perform in front of someone she thought she would never see again.

Chapter 3

Mandy saw verbena uncomfortably close to their table, and lantana crowded by the back gate. A great, hulking bush of purple lilacs stretched past August roses into the patio.

If someone didn't work on this yard soon, she expected to write an obituary about the old lady who had been swallowed alive by a Venus flytrap, like in that video she and Hilario watched about the singing dentist.

The lady, a fellow member of the Church of the Christian Revival, distributed glasses of sweet tea, then barreled back into the house. That left Mandy alone with Brother Jesse and her fellow sinners, newly roped into a prayer circle.

She thought she recognized Ricky, the surly-faced Hispanic boy—last name of Garcia?—from an article she wrote about high school artists last year, but it took Mandy a while to remember the blonde femme's name. Sherron Steinhall. She sang in the choir at church, with occasional solos.

No one was supposed to use last names in the prayer circle. Brother Jesse had stressed that rule when he had talked to her in his office. He was a thin man with graying hair swept back in an evangelist pomp. He promised not to discuss specific details of what went on in the group with her mother. He had to agree to that, given what happened the last time she tried to work with him.

The circle, he said, shouldn't be called a support group or an ex-gay ministry, because there was no such creature as a homosexual, only a confused person needing Christian fulfillment.

Brother Jesse led them in a lengthy prayer, then he opened the proceedings. "We're all sinners here. No one has a front-row ticket to heaven. Some of you are here because you want to be here. Others were encouraged to come here by family, but you're all here to learn more about becoming a fulfilled Christian. I'm glad you came."

Ricky refused to join in the scripture-reading out of the book of Romans, but Sherron took up the slack by breaking into prayer. She gathered Brother Jesse's and Mandy's hands in her own as she asked God to bring healing into everyone's lives.

Sherron seemed to understand the challenge they faced in not acting on their emotions. From the way she described it, women were throwing themselves at her right and left, and some of the passes sounded downright explicit. A local woman tried to kiss Sherron in her own swimming pool? Another one felt her up in a changing room? Mandy felt like an underachiever with only the long-ago Doris as her sin partner, and she had somehow managed to live in Tantona for twenty-eight years without getting hit on at the Dairy Queen.

Hilario refused to attend. He told her that morning when she was leaving for church he had already picked out a circle in hell in which to burn. This left her on her own, except for a tight-lipped kid, the gabby Sherron, and Brother Jesse. The pastor tried to move the meeting back to a more spiritual plane.

"I never even kissed a man." Ricky broke into Brother Jesse's discussion of how prayer warriors could help each other deal with temptation. "I've never done anything to get in trouble. I don't belong here."

"Your mother said she came across a magazine."

"It wasn't mine. It was my cousin's. I told her that, but she didn't believe me." Ricky's hands were clenched so hard on the table that they were vibrating.

Mandy remembered him at the high school art department, talking enthusiastically about his trip to a Dallas museum exhibit on abstract expressionists. At the moment, however, he looked about as cornered as a coyote in a box trap.

"Face it, you're gay," Mandy said, surprising herself by speaking up. "It's not about who you screw—sorry, Brother Jesse—it's about what you feel. You can't change that until you admit you've got a problem."

"Well, I'm not a faggot. I'm not you."

"No, you're not me."

They were all looking at Mandy. In for a penny, in for a dollar, Daddy always said.

"All I know is that I'm tired of fighting this and being so alone. I don't want to feel this way twenty years down the road knowing I didn't try to do something about it. You're just a kid. Maybe you're getting at it early enough that you can change more than me."

"It's not too late for you, Mandy," Brother Jesse said. "It's not too late for any of you, if you make an honest effort. You can be a prayer warrior for yourself and for each other. Call on the Holy Spirit to remove the source of evil in your life. Only by the grace of God can you be healed."

They joined hands as Brother Jesse led them in a round-robin prayer, during which Ricky began crying in convulsive sobs that shook his body. Tactfully, Brother Jesse didn't push him into taking a turn on praying.

Afterward, the host gave all of them hugs as they left. Mandy saw Sherron slip into a late-model Town Car driven by her husband, whose first name escaped Mandy. About the time they started coming to church was when her attendance turned spotty.

Did he push Sherron into doing this, she wondered. A fancy woman like that had a lot to lose if people in Tantona found out she was gay, unlike Mandy, who could walk into a 7-11 anytime and get hired to run the cash register and make as much money as she did at the paper. It wasn't like Mandy ever received an invitation to the country club.

Her brothers cared more about where the next beer was coming from and what girl they could talk into bed than about things that really mattered. For some reason, she'd always wanted more than that. She needed to hear something from God other than a yawning silence. She had to get this problem fixed. If she did her part, maybe God would do His.

* * *

Tina pushed back her unfinished plate of shrimp enchiladas. Abuelo's was her favorite Mexican restaurant in Lubbock, but the portions were heroic, even with her increased appetite from all the walking she'd been doing lately.

"Then my brother pulled him out of the clothes hamper where he'd been sleeping all along, and Sheila had to call the police back. My nephew is great at disappearing on a second's notice. I have to keep a sharp eye out when I'm babysitting."

Syd took a sip from her glass of sangria.

They were enjoying an early supper and resting their feet after having traipsed all over the South Plains Mall. Tina was still experiencing sticker shock, partly assuaged by her glass of sangria.

For the most part, Tina went along with everything Syd suggested while shopping, except for the Cyndi Lauper-style bangles that even she knew were out of fashion. Idly looking over to the next table, she noticed a woman sitting with a male companion. She had a Jamie Lee Curtis haircut, but a bit fuller in the back. Tina's hair, a dark brown mass hanging down her back, suddenly felt much too heavy, so unnecessary, like thick curtains hiding a picture window.

"What's going on in there?" Syd asked. "You've got a major frown going on."

"I'm thinking of getting a haircut."

"Wow, that's a serious subject. Not." They both laughed at that. "Who does your hair?"

"No one, really."

"You need to visit Neil's Better Cuts. I've been going to him for years."

Given an excuse for examining Syd, Tina noticed that the layering gave her hair life and motion. Funny how you could have basically the same length, give or take an inch, and on one person, it looked like an old army blanket, and on another person, it came off as youthful.

"I guess I'll be visiting Neil. I know it doesn't matter, but isn't he gay?"

It was a silly ploy to bring up the subject, but she was out of ideas, since her mentions of Rita Mae Brown and Martina Navratilova, and the discussion of their own poor dating histories hadn't worked.

Syd made a point of closing Tina's car door for her throughout the afternoon, carried more than her share of shopping bags, and would have hauled them all if Tina hadn't insisted on sharing the load. She behaved like a complete gentleman, Tina thought to herself, mentally subtracting the irony.

Syd snatched the bill out of Tina's hand when it arrived.

"He has a family. I don't know if he's gay."

Oh, for heaven's sake. "Would you like to go out on a date sometime?"

Syd drew the moment out by finishing off her glass of sangria. The alarm in her eyes this time seemed genuine.

"Is now okay?" she said, finally.

They sat together in a movie theater, sharing a vat of buttered popcorn at a showing of *Steel Magnolias*. They somehow managed to brush up against each other's hands and thighs several times. While watching Sally Field's falling apart scene, Tina realized that she had been crying for a while and feeling a surge of anger.

"What's the matter?" Syd asked later as they crossed the parking lot to the car.

"I hate movie death scenes. That girl was so pretty when she died." She couldn't make the words come out the way she intended.

"I don't know. There were IVs going, and the actress was real skinny. She looked sick. Sure, they staged it pure Hollywood, but I don't think your average movie audience is ready for the way the process really works. Sally Field did a good job of freaking out. That part felt genuine to me."

Syd briefly put an arm around Tina as they headed across the parking lot.

The wind blew a purple shopping bag high into the air. It curlicued downward across their path and collided with a pickup-truck window. Syd stopped with her to watch the performance. A gust of wind snagged the bag anew, gliding it upward in constant torsion.

"Go, go," Syd urged in a whisper. The bag twirled upward around a light pole, then, the wind at a standstill, dropped softly onto the hood of a nearby car.

"Nice," Tina said.

Syd started to kiss her. A regular couple came walking up to a pickup a few yards away, so she backed off, opened the car door, and Tina got in.

Once they were both inside, Syd gave her a grin. "I guess we're a pair of weirdoes, getting off on a plastic bag."

"I guess so."

They kissed, then Syd drew her into an embrace. For a contrarian moment, Tina wanted to open her door, to give anyone a free view. *Hello, human interaction taking place.*

"Let's go home." Syd's voice was soft in Tina's ear.

"I can't make any promises."

"I'm not in a hurry, are you?"

* * *

Their cat, Barry, picked his way across the lawn carefully. He paused now and then as though he had some doubt as to where he was headed, when as usual, his nose and ears were routing him directly to Wesley, currently lounging on the back-porch steps.

On Wesley's jam box, Patty Loveless sang in her worn, yet poignant voice, a tune about falling in love. It was exactly the kind of song Cat could have sung in her sleep back in her country days, and probably did.

Barry leapt through the air, landing next to Wesley, who lifted the black shorthair onto his lap and returned to his intense inspection of a racing magazine, despite the encroaching dusk.

Cat turned on the porch light and settled on a step below him to sip a limeade.

"Mom?" Wesley said in his newly acquired baritone rumble. That, and the three inches of height added seemingly overnight, reminded her that her brother had accomplished the same growth spurt in even less time.

Wesley might hold off on shaving for a while longer, but given the Talamantez bloodline, he would probably be sporting a five o'clock shadow before long, making him the world's most grizzled freshman.

"Yeah, babe?"

"Barry's having more trouble seeing."

"I know. He's getting around okay, though."

They watched Barry, his white whiskers vibrating as he burrowed farther down into Wesley's lap.

"How old is he?" Wesley asked.

"He's thirteen, but doing pretty well, considering."

"Mom?"

"Yeah?"

"Mrs. Horton wants to know if y'all can go to church with us next week."

"You know how I feel about that. I'm glad you're going, but it's not for me." Cat was a lapsed Catholic and Neil a former Southern Baptist. Neither of them believed in churches that didn't believe in them.

"Why?" Wesley laid his magazine on the porch and looked down at his mother.

He was so big now. Always a sweet, stalwart boy, he miraculously avoided the jerk phase of middle school. He recently began attending the Church of the Christian Revival with the Hortons, who all joined earlier in the year.

"Wesley, I know there's a God. I know that one-hundred percent. The thing is, I'm not comfortable with labels of any kind."

"Why? Is it because of Dad?"

"What do you mean?" She thought she already knew the answer.

Back in third grade, Wesley came to her upset over a classmate calling Neil a queer. The classmate might not have even known what the word meant, but Wesley could tell it was a bad word. Since then, Wesley knew that Neil decided to become a family man, with the details left vague.

"Dad is gay, isn't he." Wesley said it as a statement, not an inquiry.

Cat put down her drink. "He loves you and would never do anything to hurt you, but yeah, he's gay."

"I knew." Her son had an air of quiet satisfaction. "Why do you stay with him?"

Just then Barry jumped from Wesley's lap into hers. Cat stroked his fur as she collected her thoughts, thinking of all the years given her to prepare and she still didn't have a story. The truth would have to do.

"We love each other, Wes. That won't ever change."

"What happens if he meets a man, or you meet… someone?"

There in the spaces, the truth from her son. He had watched both of his parents over the years and come to certain conclusions. His conclusions happened to be correct, but at the same time, she refused to discuss intimate details with her son. He was still a kid, incipient mustache or not.

"You're number one for us, Wesley, our top priority. You always will be. We love you. I love you very much."

She gave him a kiss, returned Barry to her son's lap, and went back inside to find Neil getting off the phone with Dad. Neil got along better with her father than she did, as Dad had an opinion on every aspect of Cat's life. Currently, he took issue with her decision to form an alternative music band. Bad enough that she failed to meet his many expectations when she was younger, but now she insisted on flaunting her disreputable behavior on the road.

"Dad still at it?" She settled down on the sofa beside him. Neil promptly stole a sip from her glass.

"You know him. Juan called around to clubs in Amarillo and only found two places that would even book Blue Movie. And did he make the bookings? No. He wanted to prove how hard it would be."

"That's Dad for you."

"I called the two clubs he mentioned. I got y'all booked at one of them for October, and the other will call me back. I called Juan back to give him the news."

"How did he take it?"

"Surprisingly well. Mama sends her love."

Before he could take his video of *The Graduate* off pause, she told him of her conversation with Wesley. He nodded his head slowly.

"I've been expecting him to say something. I'll go out and talk to him."

She settled back on the sofa and thought about Dani, who had phoned again that afternoon. Neil told her to stop bothering them. Almost fifteen years had passed, and just because Cat happened to be playing at a club down the street, Dani thought she could come over and say hello, as if Cat had no reason to wish her all the heartache in the world.

That was a tale she hoped Wesley would never have to hear, about the night he was conceived, the botched relationships leading up to it, and all that followed. Someday, though, her son would want to know the rest of it, and on that day, Cat would have to admit the truth. But how, how would she tell him?

She started the story in silence, pretending the flickering image of Dustin Hoffman on the TV screen was Wesley in a few years.

"It all began when Dani asked me out."

No, it didn't start there.

"I went out with two different boys at the beginning of my senior year at Amarillo High School. I made myself have sex with them, even though it made my flesh crawl, made me almost physically ill, yet I did it because I thought I had a nervous problem. If I relaxed enough, then it wouldn't feel so alien to me, but even a six-pack of Budweiser couldn't get me going."

That was not the kind of detail one shared with a son at any point.

"Later, Dani and I dared each other to go to the gay club. We had fake IDs, but nobody asked to see them. We walked right in, and the first person I saw, it turned out, was Neil dancing with a salesman who said he was bisexual. So on the same night, Dani and I had our first night of adolescent groping at her father's house—he was out of town—and Neil decided to pursue the bisexuality his salesman said was a requirement."

That made Neil sound shallow. Infatuation makes a person do all kinds of stupid things, especially teenagers like her and Dani, or even when that person is nine years older, as with Neil, who had been dumped by his lover.

"The next weekend, Dani decided to crash a party she heard about and dragged me along. Next to the tequila sunrise punch bowl, I met Neil, both of us plastered and desperate, both of us with something to prove. Me, because Dad listened in on my phone conversation with Dani and threatened to send me to a cousin's house in New Mexico, and Neil, because the salesman made it clear that he wouldn't bother with anyone who wasn't bisexual."

Did her son really need to know all the facts? Cat told Neil she was twenty-one and just passing through town. In a boozy haze, in a shadowy back bedroom, they had hasty, unprotected sex. Each then wandered off looking for their dates. Dani was smoking cigarettes in the den with a pair of drag queens. The party had run out of steam, or maybe just out of tequila.

The next day, her hangover making the sunlight feel like a blowtorch, she told her father that she was completely, totally heterosexual. No further explanation sought, none offered.

The story couldn't possibly be helpful to her son's emotional development. His parents conceived him on a night of less-than-unbridled lust, and if not for a matter of timing, would never have seen each other again.

"I'm thinking I'm safe, because an act so sickening couldn't possibly unite my egg with a sperm. So silly, and then so desperate, haunting the bar until someone told me Neil's last name. I showed up crying at his apartment."

If she wanted to scare her son into lifelong abstinence, she would tell him every unpleasant detail, even the part where a rattled Neil drove her to a doctor with a reputation of doing abortions for hire. He stayed by her side in the doctor's office as she came to the realization that she couldn't go through with it.

Her girlfriend proved to be a non-factor throughout the whole ordeal. Dani's mother promised Dani a car if she agreed to move with her to Lubbock. For the payoff of a Pontiac Fiero, she vanished from Cat's life.

"Neil invited me to move in with him when Dad kept pushing me to go to the unwed mother's home in San Antonio. One morning while I was cooking an omelet, Neil proposed. I took the first mature step in my life when I rode with him to a justice of the peace."

Yes, end with the positive points. Despite the wrong-headed reasons—the salesman moved to Denver with the most effeminate man in Amarillo, if not Texas, while Cat knew, even as she was giving birth, she had no interest in ever repeating the act that landed her in stirrups—despite all that, she saw Neil's concerned face and knew she'd made the right decision. He became her husband by law and by heart.

That's how she would talk to her son, if she ever decided to tell him more than a bare line of her autobiography. Maybe someday she might want a romantic relationship, but until that unlikely event, she had Neil, except for his occasional weekends in Dallas. He wasn't a saint.

Neil came in and sat back down, taking a sip from her long-melted limeade.

"How did it go?"

"Not bad. He did ask if I'm his birth father. That's the way he put it. I told him I'm his birth father, his all-the-way-to-the-grave, kick-his-butt-when-he-misbehaves father. It seemed to get the point across. And, he wants us to go to church with him. I explained to him that I'm okay with my current level of spiritual commitment, which I hope satisfies him."

"For now," Cat said. "Felix and Marta have gotten so gung-ho about church these days. Wesley always takes his cue from the whole Horton clan. Drag racing, and now church."

"It could be worse, you know. They could be Satanists or wife-swappers. At least he's getting positive experiences from them."

"Yeah, from a conventional mother and father."

"He could use a more masculine influence."

"I think you're a great father."

"Thank you, Caterina." He took the video off pause.

Dustin was about to receive a lewd proposal from Anne Bancroft. Hets.

Chapter 4

"There ain't no reason to get excited about a little dust these days, 'cause back when I was a child, it weren't nothing for the wind to come lay a foot of sand in the kitchen. I remember Mother taking a shovel to push it on out the door. If she raised a blister, you wouldn't know it. I never heard her complain one bit. People don't hardly know what it's like. They don't know how it used to be around here."

Mandy listened as the speaker of those comments sat near the entrance to the nursing home, his shoulders stooped and his unlikely black hair spread in patchy islands from the back of his neck to his widower's peak. There was a shiny layer of pomade bridging enough strands to keep the structure from total collapse.

Throughout her interview with Maitland Deakins, Mandy tried to avoid staring at his, well, *hair* seemed too strong a word. A hair-like substance, perhaps.

"You got a cigarette on you?"

"Sorry, no."

"It's a filthy habit," he said with a triumphal air. "Takes years off your life. I'm ninety-four years of age, don't you know. I'd uh planned on a flat hundred, but on account of Demon Weed, I'm not thinking I'll get past ninety-six."

Afterward, she drove over to Gardner's Steak House, a place Sherron Steinhall mentioned in their morning phone call as where she wanted to meet for lunch. Mandy had looked up Sherron's family in the city directory. Husband: Ryan. Daughter: Emily. They lived on the expensive end of Phipps Avenue.

Sherron, who was waiting by the cashier's desk, wore a turquoise silk dress with three-quarter sleeves, her makeup fastidiously done. Her appearance served as further reminder that the two of them traveled in different social brackets.

It also occurred to Mandy that Sherron's hair had something in common with Mr. Deakins's do. Both ranked as technical achievements. Sherron's chic style—no matronly bubble for her—covered all but a hint of brunette roots.

She was slightly taller than Mandy, with the fine-boned angularity of a woman on a permanent diet, and blessed with a flawless, lightly tanned complexion and azure eyes. Sherron led them to the buffet.

"We both have offices to get back to. I figure we can get the meal out of the way and have more time to talk." But then she dawdled on the buffet line, waving at apparent friends she saw eating around the restaurant.

"If anyone asks, you're doing an article about my collection of crystal figurines," she whispered.

No one asked. Halfway through her salad, Sherron brought up why they were eating together. She had been absorbed in explaining some obscure point of Medicare coverage she couldn't make clear to one of the doctors. Mandy couldn't understand it, either.

"Oh good, the Inkstons left." A sour-faced older couple had been sitting two tables over by the window.

"What you need to know, Mandy, is I'm not really that way. My husband happened to overhear me on the phone and got the wrong idea. I'm seeing Brother Jesse so Ryan will get back to trusting me, that's all."

"You sound really experienced."

Sherron puffed her cheeks out in exasperation as she distractedly pushed a piece of broccoli around with her fork.

"Once or twice, I did get kind of involved with people. Ryan knows all about it. He and Brother Jesse think I've been backsliding, so I'm stuck going to the prayer circle until they believe I've mended my ways. I might as well have some fun with it."

She flashed a mischievous smile. "I've been singing for years about Jesus washing away my sins, so let's make them spicy. If Brother Jesse asks you, we're praying our little hearts out."

"Well, I am praying my heart out. I want to change. It's not an act with me."

"Is it true you've only been with one other person?" Sherron glanced furtively at their surroundings as she spoke.

"Yes."

"You look really gay. I thought you'd been around more." She seemed disappointed.

"What does gay look like?"

"Don't be offended. You don't wear makeup, except for lip gloss. Even in church, you wear slacks, and you walk kind of tough."

"So? I like keeping it simple."

Everything about Sherron, her ultra-pristine look, her pushiness, her anxiety about being seen with a lesbian—it all grated on Mandy until she let loose.

"Do you really think you're not gay? That you're not a lesbian?"

Sherron's eyes widened in fear as she checked the nearest table. There, a quartet of Halliburton workers was holding forth about their new boss.

Mandy took her voice down a notch to keep Sherron from bolting. "I don't know if it's possible to change, if God has that in store for me. I don't know how many people you've been with, and I don't care. It's in you, and you're not going to get it out without help."

Anger showed in Sherron's eyes as she fidgeted with her glass of tea. "You make it sound like I have a tumor, something that's going to kill me. Let me assure you, I am alive and well. I'm a good wife, despite what my husband thinks right now, and I'm a good mother. I'll pray with you, because despite what you think, I believe in prayer. I just don't think it's a big deal. Heck, look at the Inkstons. They go to our church. Ryan says that man has his hand in more crooked deals—"

"I don't care."

"And his wife, you ought to hear her talk. She's real prejudiced."

"I don't give a rip, Sherron. It's their lives, not mine. People can be hypocrites in and out of church. That don't matter to me. I just know the Bible says I'm going to hell. The end. I've tried on my own to change, I've tried to live with it, I've tried to smoke my way through it. I can't figure out anything else to do, except this."

She couldn't keep her voice from shaking. This time Sherron's gaze stayed on her.

"Neither can I." Her voice was almost inaudible.

* * *

"Jamie Lee Curtis, you say?" Neil Acuff ran his fingers through Tina's hair. "Are you sure you want it that short?"

Tina sat in the swivel chair, waiting for whatever magic the man possessed, and wishing she felt more on top of the situation. Mary Eckert probably welcomed having some uninterrupted phone time at Tina's desk to conduct her real-estate business, so why not burn off some comp time on a slower-than-usual Monday afternoon?

Something in his bearing seemed a touch soft, but no more so than some of the local ministers. However, his gelled and intricately curled hair wouldn't rest comfortably on the head of a small town suit-wearer.

Neil's Better Cuts, an airy cedar and glass building next door to a run-down magneto shop, lacked the humid chemical presence of the beauty shops her mother took her to when she was a girl. Neil hummed along absentmindedly to a country tune as he considered her head.

"Yes," Tina said. "Maybe a little shorter in the back, but yes."

"You do have the head for it."

"What do you mean?"

A lithe woman Tina recognized came through the door, carrying several plastic food containers. Cat Acuff, a friendly library patron who liked foreign authors. They often talked in the stacks about books and movies—every topic under the sun, it seemed like—yet somehow Cat never mentioned a husband.

"Some people's heads are too broad, too rounded, so they look like bowling balls in short hair. It's best if your head is a bit narrow, but not too narrow, and that your face is either oval or heart-shaped with delicate features, then you look prettier."

"You don't look too butch, is what my husband's saying." Cat began opening containers and divvying out portions of Chinese food as she spoke. "Hi, Tina."

"Hi." They were married. For some reason, she had never connected the two.

One of the other hairdressers, a woman with strange pale hair, said edgily, "I hope you don't mind. We were listening to country music."

"It's the Maines Brothers. At least they have some attitude. And y'all listen to what you want." Cat continued loading plates. "Neil, I'm splitting the sweet and sour pork between you and the others."

"Caterina, just keep me supplied with egg rolls. That's all I care about." He spritzed Tina's hair with water from a bottle.

Tina learned a few things over the next few minutes: that a previously soft-voiced Cat turned up her volume outside the library, that China Land hired a new cook, that Cat might say she liked country music but almost instantly popped in a tape of edgy sounding rock, that Neil worked fast, and that her head, however shaped, had lost about five pounds.

Neil whipped off her cover. "There you are—a brand new woman."

Tina tilted her head in different angles as she examined herself in the mirror. She got up slowly as Neil joined his wife at a table near the cashier desk. Feeling dazed, she dropped a twenty on the table.

"We owe you change," Cat said, rising on her words. "Did you not like your cut? He can do some more on it."

"No, it's fine. You don't owe me anything. I'll see you next time you come into the library." Tina walked out the door.

Neil was right about the shape of her head. Tina stared into her rearview mirror. She realized how much she resembled her brother; that is, if Jack had survived into his forties with both mind and body intact. He never had that chance.

In her shoes, what would he have made of his life by now? Would he be the teacher he talked about, the basketball player, the actor? He had so many dreams and never got to live out a single one. What did she have to say in her defense, that she had been afraid all this time of possibilities out of her control?

She put the car in gear and headed for Syd's house. Syd, dressed in a tank and cutoffs, was sweeping out the garage.

"Sorry, I can't stay long. I need to get back to work." Tina spun around to display her new haircut.

Syd shook her head as she walked back inside the house.

On her heels, Tina asked, "What's the matter?"

Syd chunked the broom in the hall closet then went into the kitchen and fixed a glass of ice water. She took a long swallow. "Would you like a glass?"

"No. What's the matter?" Syd could not look at her. "I told you I was getting a haircut. You said it was a good idea."

"Not that short. What with the outfits you have now, you're going to look too masculine."

"You picked out half my clothes."

"You look better with those sorts of lines, but you can't go too far with the rest of it. You need to wear more makeup, and the hair has to fit in." Syd's face had a closed-off expression as she sat down at the kitchen table.

"Half the women in town have hair this short. I'm not going to poof it up, that's all. What the hell is going on? What's the problem? Look at me, Syd."

"Tommy broke up with me this morning. Again. He was heading out to the farm, he said, so he couldn't talk long." Syd frowned and slid a sand dollar coaster under her glass.

"So? You were pretending to be a couple. It wasn't for real."

"Real enough for his parents, real enough for my coworkers. Now, I don't have anyone."

"You have me. I thought." They'd shared kisses, with the unspoken promise of more to come.

Syd managed a timid smile. "A few years ago, there was a woman hired at the Middle School. They said she showed up for the interview in a dress, but after that she had on man-cut pants. I remember seeing her. An out-and-out dyke, and cute."

Syd brightened at the memory, then her smile vanished. "She didn't get hired back the next year."

"Was she a good teacher?"

"From what I heard, yes, but it doesn't matter. The principal, he brought her in at some point and asked if she was a lesbian. Parents were complaining about the way she looked. She said yes, so he had grounds to fire her right then, but he let her stay through the end of the school year. He wanted her to be able to find another job somewhere."

"How nice of him," Tina said sarcastically.

"Actually, yes. I'm not sure Mr. Tickner would extend the same courtesy in my case." Syd mimicked that fussbudget's phrasing, who was well if not fondly remembered by Tina from her years as a history teacher.

"So this is all about you being afraid of getting fired for breaking some stupid law."

"You should be worried, too."

A few inches of hair and Tommy Williams calling off the charade. How petty, how huge. She had no idea until that moment how big the stakes were to Syd.

"This is what I'll do. I'll make sure I have makeup on, that I wear enough jewelry. I won't mention you at work. I'll lay low. Will that work?" Tina knew she sounded panicked, but she couldn't seem to stop it. "Or, do you want us to stop seeing each other?"

Syd rose from her chair and pulled Tina into her arms.

* * *

By mid-afternoon, Cat pronounced herself ready for a break. It took longer than usual to complete her client work, as one of her truck drivers had made a mess of his receipts.

"Neil," she called to him at the back of the shop, where he was rinsing out a customer's hair. "I'm going to check on Wesley. Do you need anything?"

"No. Make sure he weed-eats the alley. He forgot last time."

At the door she met Mimi Dimmells, Kentrell's older sister, who was dressed in her jailer uniform. She went back inside with Mimi, whose smooth face and quiet demeanor gave no indication of her line of work. Kentrell said she could take down a prisoner without breaking a nail, much less a sweat. Mimi didn't waste any time getting to her subject.

"I'm sure Kentrell's too embarrassed to call you, but our parents don't want him in the band anymore."

"Why?" While a good musician and on time for rehearsals, Kentrell couldn't remember a lyric to save his life and carried a tune as though it was a burden. Still, he had sworn that his upcoming senior year of high school posed no scheduling problems.

"It's a religious thing. I guess they heard about the drinking and some of the places you were planning to play. Our mother, if you want to know the truth, said she wasn't about to let him do it anymore. But I have a solution. I don't know if Kentrell told you, but I've been listening to y'all's rehearsal tapes, and you know I was there at the show. I'm comfortable with your songs, and it wouldn't be any problem for me to step in."

Cat vaguely remembered Kentrell saying that his sister used to play in church. It wouldn't hurt just to see. Cat took her to the back rehearsal room, and by the time she turned on the equipment, Mimi was ready at the keys.

Mimi kicked off with a song Cat recognized from a Linda Ronstadt album, "I Still Miss Someone," written by Johnny Cash. Cat heard an interesting mix of soul and country in Mimi's voice, and unlike her brother, she could actually sing. After a verse and chorus, Mimi stopped and looked at her expectantly.

"We're not a country band, but if you don't mind that, I'd love for you to join us."

Mimi left the shop after they worked out the schedule.

Cat walked past Neil, who was sweeping the floor. She took the broom out of his hands and finished up while Neil opened a new container of roller papers.

"I defy anyone to cause a commotion at your shows. That gal can shut them down in a hurry."

"Oh, Neil. She's not big."

"She's bigger than you. And rather attractive." He waggled an eyebrow at her as his next client entered.

"Oh, you think you have competition?" Cat felt safe in giving it back to him. His staff had left for the day.

"I wouldn't call it that, but you ought to think about, you know, those kind of options. You've waited a long time." He greeted his client, an elderly blue-hair. "Let's get you in the chair, sweetheart. I don't know if I can possibly improve on perfection, but I'll try."

Cat glared at her husband, who refused to meet her eyes. Why was he talking up Mimi, a woman she hardly knew?

Thinking back to earlier, she recalled Tina's expression, as though she had seen a stranger in the mirror. Some clients acted that way after an appointment. Cat saw Tina as a still-waters-run-deep kind of person. Maybe that's why she enjoyed talking with Tina at the library, just to see those moments when her librarian shared in a laugh. Tina had a wide smile and clear green eyes—eyes that had seemed stunned earlier.

She set aside the broom and walked closer to the mirror. What would she see now? Behind her, the clock's reflection reminded her of Wesley and the weed-eater. She rolled her eyes and sighed, then chuckled at the expression she made.

First Wesley, and then her husband, the matchmaker.

Chapter 5

Tuesdays, more often than not, saw Hilario home in time for a sit-down supper. They both had erratic evening schedules, what with Mandy having to cover school board meetings, football Fridays, election nights, and random news events. Circumstances conspired to make Mandy feel she was at the beck and call of an entire town.

Someone had to do it. Someone had to help render a twice-a-week, shallow, inaccurate, yet technically correct version of Tantona, just as someone needed to cook enchilada plates. Both of them performed necessary services, although she believed Hilario got the better end of the deal. If people didn't like their food, they sent back the plate. They didn't write angry letters to the editor or haunt the publisher's office.

"Your girlfriend called." Hilario sliced onions with his usual flair. He didn't like to stand over the stove, but he always did the chopping, saying that Mandy took too much time.

"Girlfriend?"

"Okay, your prayer partner. I checked her out yesterday when I went to see my aunt in the hospital. I hung around near the business office until I could see the nameplate on her desk. She's pretty. She has about a million pictures of her family, but maybe she can make room for one of you."

"She's not my lover."

"I think y'all would look cute together, putting your heads together and praying, like that does anything." He dumped the onions in the skillet and moved on to the garlic cloves. "How did the meeting this afternoon go?"

"It went better than I expected. I might get a raise the first of the year."

Sherron, saying Mandy was paid worse than a field hand, coached her on how to approach her boss. If that didn't work, she thought she could get Mandy in as a phlebotomist trainee. From there, she could work toward becoming a lab technician.

"Isn't it nice you have a connection at the hospital?"

Their daily clashes were now down to occasional cutting remarks. He no longer ran his stereo full blast when he knew she was praying or reading the Bible, and she, in turn, didn't try to talk him into attending the prayer circle.

"Sherron isn't doing anything more than what a friend would do."

"You've been to her house when her family wasn't there." He dumped the chopped garlic in the skillet along with another splash of olive oil.

"And nothing happened." Given how intimidated Mandy felt by the drapes of Sherron's upscale home, she couldn't have made a move on Sherron if her life depended on it.

"It will. She'll get to you, and she won't even know she's doing it. She can't help it, you can't help it. Sex happens. Oh, excuse me, love happens." He smirked as he sprinkled comino, salt, and black pepper in the pan.

Who would want to be gay based on his attitude, she thought, and said as much.

"True, *mija*, it's true. You want something different? Move. Me, now that I'm in a decent place, I can start saving money. I'm not staying here."

If he brought up San Antonio again, he'd be eating by himself. Her lack of interest must have shown on her face.

"We have no business being here. You're getting sucked into some kind of cult, and me, I'm getting gray hair dealing with that plowboy. I swear I'm really going to move this time. We both need to get out of town. Oh, and Erma Delgado split up with Mickey Reyes. Word is she didn't want to put out. You could have nailed her."

Mandy finished salting and spicing the chicken strips, then dropped them into the sizzling oil. "Erma might be gay, but I'm not into any kind of bar scene anymore."

"You got it all confused." Hilario spoke as patiently as she had ever heard him. Minced jalapeno flew into the pan, followed by the contents of a can of chopped green chilies.

"You don't want to smoke bud or drink Bud, that's one thing, but doing the ladies, that's not a sin. You need to find someone you want to stay with—that's how you girls do it—then forget about that *guera chingalera*. Sherron and Brother Jesse, they're going to screw up your head. You can't let that happen. Now don't forget the *crema*."

* * *

High school teacher in-service started next week, which meant Syd would soon be back into the classroom. That meant less time for her and Tina to work on their relationship, if one could grace such a frail flower with the word.

Mary Eckert happened to be at the desk once when Syd checked in her books and saw something, maybe a look that passed between Syd and Tina, because Mary then renewed her invitation to the Eckerts' annual October party.

"Bring Sydney with you. The more the merrier. We even have Jim's band playing. That Acuff woman sings with them. The two of you get along pretty well, looks like. And LaSonda's mother, Barbara, is coming." Mary said the last name with particular emphasis.

Barbara Wolfe, the local notorious lesbian, had been married during the last ice age to Barlow Eckert's brother. LaSonda Kindred, an RN at the hospital, recently reconciled with her mother.

Tina placed thoughts of that conversation far into the background and returned to the night's business of touching Syd. According to Syd's unspoken ground rules, Tina needed to be out the door soon, but the sofa, cool jazz, and caresses—what sane person would want to leave? What sane person would not be in bed at this moment, continuing the physical dialogue?

She stood up and said quietly, "Let's go."

Syd looked nervous to the point of being ill, but she followed Tina into the bedroom.

They started undressing separately, but then Syd came up behind her and unclasped her bra, kissing her on the nape of her neck. Syd lowered Tina to the bed.

As she stretched underneath Syd, who still had only shed her T-shirt, Tina tried to unclothe her, but in a few quick moves, Syd accomplished the task on her own. She returned to kissing Tina on the neck, moving steadily downward. Tina tried to respond, but Syd subtly and not so subtly thwarted her moves.

"Just lay back and let me do it," Syd whispered.

She started to tell her no, to just get up and leave, but she didn't. It had been so long since anyone had touched her that she settled for what she could get, no matter how one-sided the transaction.

Afterward, they dressed in silence. She wanted to talk about what had just happened, but Syd appeared completely absorbed by looking out through the living room curtains for signs of traffic on the street. The coast clear, Tina left for home.

Syd never came to her place. She claimed that the duplex walls were too thin. Tina thought it obvious that Syd didn't want Becca to see the two of them together. Tina told her that Becca probably wouldn't care, which prompted Syd to again extract a promise from Tina that she would remain quiet about their relationship.

Tina supposed one could call it a relationship, but after what happened, how could they be described as partners? There was no equality between them; there was only giver and recipient.

They had yet to eat together publicly anywhere in Tantona, as Syd preferred grilling steaks or their dining on Chinese or Mexican take-out. She was afraid they would be spotted by coworkers or her siblings, or cousins, or church members, or anyone.

There was something to be said for Tina having no family at all, save for her father in Houston. The only relative she ever met was her grandmother—her father's mother, who came up for a visit when Tina was around fourteen years old. That marked the first time Tina ever witnessed the look, for she applied it to Mom the entire time she was there. Mrs. Ransom was a tall, spare woman with dyed black hair who couldn't get a word out edgewise without Dad speaking gruffly to her. He kept finding errands for Jack and Tina to do that kept them away from this stranger who was supposed to be their grandmother, but the afternoon before she left, she took Tina aside and told her, "They had no right to do this to you, no right at all." She stared fearfully at Tina, tears streaming down her face. She never came back again.

Syd at least never applied any kind of look to Tina, even though she seemed not to want to see her at times. Her paranoia was starting to infect Tina, as these days she took entirely too much time getting ready for work.

That morning, she had debated how many buttons should be buttoned on her new silk fuchsia blouse and how exactly to roll up the sleeves. She left the apartment with a fair amount of cleavage on display, along with the gold heart necklace Syd had given her last week.

Syd wanted their relationship classified, yet so far, she had given Tina a necklace, a potted plant, a dozen roses, and she sent over a cookie pizza for the library staff last Saturday, no name attached. Even businesslike Otilia asked about Tina's mystery man, which meant that Mary must have diagnosed Tina and Syd as a couple in the making. It would be a good idea not to mention that to Syd, who would go ballistic.

She felt an attraction to Syd, but to call it love would be something of a stretch. Maybe it's that she wanted to love, wanted to be close to someone, and there stood Syd, who seemed like a long, cool drink in the desert. Tina still felt parched.

* * *

Jim counted them off into another run at "Red Rocket," a band original that was supposed to be moody but now had a Mimi-supplied brightness bordering on perky. Jim, who preferred Suicidal Tendencies, complained that they were beginning to sound like the B-52s, a sentiment the ever-morose Marco seconded, yet on this, the fifth try, Cat could sense everyone getting on board.

The band needed changes of pace in the set. Thanks to Mimi, they had a fuller, more supple sound, and thanks to Neil's skill at booking, they would have plenty of chances to show it off.

They'd already played four gigs, with the next one scheduled next Saturday at Risqué, the gay club. There had been no complaints thus far from the band about the location. They were getting paid $50 apiece, plus free drinks. Throw in IHOP afterward, which Neil promised, and what could be better? A little B-52s would probably go over well at Risqué. She saw no point in mentioning that to the guys.

Cat had no intention of being as frazzled as she had been that second set at the Rattletrap. If Dani dared to show up, Cat refused to give her the thrill of a visible reaction. Now, if she could figure out what was going on with Neil. He recently deposited yet another remark about Mimi—something about how the two women could make all kinds of beautiful music together.

While she did find Mimi attractive, she wasn't going to jump her keyboard player's bones based on her husband's recommendation, which counted as a weird enough statement in its own right.

The last time Neil had been so persistent about bringing a woman to her attention, it was at the hospital a couple of years ago when Wesley went in for an appendectomy. Neil swore that the

Steinhall woman in the business office was checking Cat out, when it could well have been a name-that-fashion-label moment.

Mimi was singing on autopilot now, nowhere near full throat, but very much on pace, pacing being the main problem with the rhythm section. Marco wanted to lag a bit, a la Black Sabbath, which caused Jim to follow Marco.

Mimi stood up and signaled for them to stop. "Jim," she said without raising her voice, without the slightest hint of danger or retribution, but all the men, Jim included, froze.

"Don't ever slow down on me again. I won't have it."

She sat back down and the song started again from that point. Jim didn't slow down.

Presence, Cat thought, she has presence. Cat stole looks at her as she sang, admiring her delicate cheekbones and almond-shaped eyes, eyes disinclined to meet her gaze. Do I want her, Cat wondered? Would I give myself permission to feel such an emotion?

Turning away, she signaled Vonn to take another solo. When in doubt, jam.

> Do you remember dreaming of the
> Most wonderful, marvelous thing?
> A red rocket in the window,
> There for you, plastic joy.
> Play with your miracle toy.
> And now, and now any morning
> You wake up, you wake up together alone.
> Some strange freedom.
> What could be yours—don't know it.
> Brilliant surprise—can't see it.
> Red rocket in the window.
> The gift you never had.
> Red rocket in the window.
> Remember, remember.

Chapter 6

Five women surrounded the bridal honoree, pretending to hand her presents she had already opened and cooed over at length. Mandy snapped three photographs then wrote down their names from left to right.

Sherron, dressed in silver-embroidered white jeans and an eggshell blue scoop top, stood by the back door of the Precinct One party house. Mandy wasn't sure whether she should acknowledge Sherron on her way out. Then Momma caught up to her before she could make up her mind.

"Would you like to come to Sunday dinner?" Her mother smoothed out a wrinkle in her yellow print dress.

How did she wangle an invite to the shower? The Gabriels were miles from Judge Walt and Roberta Burlow's social set.

"Brother Jesse says you're doing real good. Daddy thought you might like to come over. We're having pot roast."

"It's okay, Mandy." Sherron stepped forward. "I can tell Ryan you had to eat with your family. I know you wanted to meet his brother-in-law."

Momma folded easily. "You can come over next Sunday, Amanda. I wouldn't want you to miss out on being with your church friends."

She faded back into the kitchen, which answered one question. Sherron's lack of fear in talking to her answered the other.

"Thank me, Amanda," Sherron said as they walked to Mandy's car.

"Only my mother calls me that, and thank you, Sherron."

"Amanda's a pretty name."

"It's not me."

"You don't know that. You might be an Amanda through and through if you gave yourself a chance. And it's bad enough I have to go to these things, why do you? Don't y'all have a photographer at the paper?"

"It's not manly enough for him, so I'm always stuck with Saturday morning showers."

"That's why you ought to get in with the hospital. You'd get scheduled some for evenings and weekends, but you'd know it in advance and get paid like you're worth something."

Sherron kept Mandy from closing the car door. She reapplied her banana clip, some strands of hair having come loose.

"Well? Are you going to do it?"

"Okay, fine. I'll go by before work Monday and fill out an application. And what's this about Ryan's brother?"

"He runs a company in Jal, New Mexico. Ryan and him never talk, but you know, he could show up for Sunday dinner sometime, and Jesus might come walk on my swimming pool. I have high hopes." She giggled.

"You have a lip on you. I don't see how you get away with it."

Mandy gave up on closing her door. Somewhere, maybe from a nearby house, she could hear a radio playing gospel music. She needed to focus on the song telling her about nail-scarred hands, and not on the living, unmarked woman in front of her.

"Mandy, I don't talk like that to anyone except you. Jesus turned water into wine. I think he liked a good time as well as anyone, but people around here don't think so."

"Maybe they have a different idea of what a good time is, and who's to say they're wrong?"

"You're a nice person, you really are, and I bet you were nice before you decided to play straight." Sherron's face turned serious. "You know everything Brother Jesse is about to say before he says it, and I think most of the time you believe it, but you shouldn't hold on to it so hard. It'll be that much harder for you when you fall off the wagon."

"Who says I will?" Sherron did not know when to shut up.

"You're human, and you don't have a husband to keep you busy. You don't have anything in your head except praying and working. You can't live on that. Look, I'm taking Emily shopping in Lubbock, but this evening two of her friends are coming over to go swimming. Why don't you come? Ryan's on call, so odds are he won't get in our hair. Don't look at me that way. They're about to go into the seventh grade. You think I could get away with some nooky with them hovering around? Well?"

"I don't think it's a good idea."

"You've been over before. Why don't you trust me?"

"I haven't been over at night."

"You don't trust yourself. That's more like it."

Sherron slammed the car door shut and left tiny dust clouds with every step back to the party. She didn't look back.

Back home, Mandy changed into blue jean shorts and did some vacuuming, although the carpet was already spotless. After a while, she called in an order to China Land and drove over to pick it up.

As she waited to pull back into traffic, she watched people going in and out of Neil Acuff's salon, which to her gave the impression of being a lawyer's office. Next to it stood her parents' business, looking shabby by comparison. A thorough washing of the plate-glass windows couldn't help but improve the appearance of the place. That, and maybe a firebombing.

Douglas was unlikely to lift a cleaning rag, even though lately he was putting in more time at the shop. His experiment at sharing a trailer with Jimmy didn't work out, according to Momma, who mentioned there had been a dispute over a long-distance phone bill. Momma swore Douglas would be moving back in with his girlfriend by the end of the month. That could happen.

Women had a way of forgiving Douglas. Mandy couldn't, not if he was going to keep breaking Momma's heart and getting arrested for stupid things like peeing outside a bar and starting fights. Daddy's favorite phrase was *que sera, sera,* believing that if Douglas ended up in prison, that was his choice to make.

Mrs. Acuff came walking out the door, which kept Mandy from recalling her family's arrest record. Those long, tanned legs. She occasionally visited the newspaper to run ads for the salon. There was something about her, perhaps the athletic bearing, that made Mandy wonder—no, she wasn't supposed to have thoughts like that, not anymore.

Mandy averted her eyes, then turned the wheel to home.

Before she rededicated her life to Christ, Mandy would have taken a second glance, noticed an attraction, but that would have been it. Now, aware that she had to follow Brother Jesse's advice and do conscious battle at all times, seeing a pretty woman could push her to the brink of exhaustion. Why did it have to be so hard?

* * *

Tina strode over to the public restroom, which was located next to the library entrance. She had looked forward to a busy Saturday afternoon, but for one, why was Mr. McBride still in town, and for another, why would he be locked in the restroom for two hours not responding to knocks on the door?

Otilia led the way. "I was fixing to call the cops, but I thought I'd wait on you."

It could be that Otilia missed seeing the man leave or he forgot to leave the door unlocked. Tina rapped her knuckles on the door and called out his name. No answer.

"Bring me the butter knife. It's in the kitchenette drawer."

Otilia scurried off. As she waited, George Bering, the library board president, came through the entrance.

"My dearest Tina." His pink, cherubic face glowed. "You're looking quite lovely today. Are those Rockies you have on?"

"As a matter of fact, yes."

She was wearing jeans, a dressy blouse, and boat shoes. Her extensive makeover routine had been reduced to stud earrings and a touch of lipstick.

Tina didn't feel like wearing drag anymore, didn't feel like making any kind of effort whatsoever to fit in, despite (or maybe because of) her phone call to Syd before she left for work.

Once again, Syd made excuses for not coming to the apartment, and once again Tina didn't push the proposal. But then, while Syd was describing a video she'd picked out for them to watch, Tina realized she couldn't stand another evening buried behind Syd's curtains. "Watch it by yourself," she told her and hung up without waiting for an answer.

Otilia breathlessly arrived, a butter knife in hand. Tina first learned her lock-picking skills as a teenager when Mom kept losing her house key. This door proved to be no challenge.

Mr. McBride had been in the middle of shaving. He lay crumpled, blue-faced, on the floor.

"George, would you go make the call for me?" Tina asked calmly.

He delivered a brief prayer, then took himself to the desk. Tina turned around to see Otilia sitting on the floor.

"Are you okay?"

"I've just seen a dead man. What do you think?"

Later on, Tina sat at her desk talking to Mary, who came into the office upon hearing the news. She had closed the library for the day and sent Otilia home.

Mary didn't seem surprised. "I wondered why he hadn't left already. He'd been moving slow the past few days. I even lined him up a free visit with Dr. Schaust, but he wouldn't go. McBride knew something was going on. He took a fast train out. Do you have any plans for the evening?"

Tina felt confused by the abrupt shift in topics. "I'm thinking of going to Lubbock or something like that."

"Good. You need to see to yourself, Tina. No one else will." Mary had an almost feral smile.

"Pardon?"

Sometimes Mary made about as much sense as an aside in Beckett, not that one of his plays was likely to be staged in Tantona.

"Jim's band is playing a club in Lubbock tonight. You need to go hear Cat Acuff sing. Barlow Eckert and I aren't going—it's bridge night at the Rosens—but if anyone should kick up their heels, Lord knows it's you."

On the way into Lubbock, Tina debated the night's plan. She hadn't reacted when Mary said that Blue Movie was performing at a gay club. She responded with a smile and said she might think about going.

True, she couldn't call Cat a close friend, but they'd known each other for years, and why on earth hadn't she figured out before that Neil and Cat were a couple?

Tina drove off the Loop onto Fourth Street, stopping at a convenience store where she bought a Coke and tried to regroup.

It took three trips around a nearby block to make sure she had the right location. Risqué had the look of a furniture warehouse gone to seed, with dreary outdoor lighting, and there were potholes in a gravel parking lot across the street.

The bars in Austin, where Tina spent one year in college before transferring to Texas Tech, might have been easier to find, but she remembered them as having an unliberated crowd of old drunks and college kids who didn't mix with each other.

Maybe the memory reflected her perspective from being a troubled nineteen-year-old at the time, unable to see happy granola gays all over the place.

She tried to drive away, tried so hard to give herself a reason to leave. She wasn't as paranoid as Syd, but Tina felt the same fear to an almost paralyzing degree.

It helped that she didn't teach at the school anymore, so getting fired wouldn't be a matter brought up at a school board meeting. Instead, County Judge Walt Burlow would call her into his office, ask in his kindly voice if there was something she needed to reveal, and that would be it.

Why not lose her job if that was the price for seeing Cat Acuff perform? She remembered seeing Cat at the King's Pub years ago with a country band. Although she sang okay, the rest of the band lacked a certain, Tina didn't know what, *joie de vivre?* Perhaps rock music made a better fit to her talent.

Go, damn it; just go inside and get it over with.

"She's awesome," Tina hollered a few minutes later to the man standing next to her. Deafened, he seemed to agree. This time, Cat's band matched her intensity, although the bass player needed a dose of caffeine.

She managed to peel herself off the wall and worked her way toward the bar, which was no easy task in a packed, sweaty house.

She felt someone take her hand. It was Neil Acuff, wearing a great grin on his face. He wiggled them closer to the band, stepping on more than a few toes along the way, until he dug them a choice spot next to the stage. Turning to holler thanks, she instead saw a large girl bouncing up and down with the beat.

She had no idea Cat could be so explosive, so wrought up. The band launched into "Voices Carry." Tina thought, here's a song the crowd will enjoy, but where Aimee Mann seemed pissed off, Cat sounded off with a righteous, soulful fury, calling down the gods for vengeance, all this with a body hard to ignore. Amazing.

* * *

Five minutes of sound check, and they were ready to roll. Cat had seen no sign of Dani, but it was still early. The guys in the band had already knocked down a round of beers, with Marco still asking cautiously, "And it's free, right?"

It was safe to say no one from Tantona would be cheering them on tonight, not in a gay bar, but Cat recognized some faces from their earlier shows. They were gay or gay-unafraid, whichever, and much appreciated.

For tonight, Cat decided to go with a black leather mini and a tight, maybe too tight, scarlet top. She had practiced all week walking on a new pair of spiked heels and felt fairly comfortable. There would be no fancy moves tonight, however, if she wanted to keep her butt from hitting the floor.

She could see pockets of lesbians at the pool tables and a large group of collegiate boys already parked in tables near the dance floor. A cloud of cigarette smoke hung in the air.

Kicking off, the band sailed confidently through their cover of The Cure's "Why Can't I Be You?" which inspired only one couple to dance. Then midway through their fourth song of the set, a throng of writhing people materialized on the dance floor. Fans didn't bother waiting for the break, for there were drinks and a loaded tip jar lined up on the bandstand in front of Cat's microphone.

Vonn's patter about giving the people what they wanted seemed to be going on longer than usual, so Cat handed off a gift drink to Mimi, who said, shielding her microphone, "Thanks, Miss Moneybags."

"I'm splitting the tips with y'all."

"Put the cash toward buying you more clothes, since you're too broke to afford any."

"Listen, I'm well covered." She realized at that moment that Vonn had quit talking and Jim was counting off.

They performed a cover of "Voices Carry," with a big stick from Jim. As she sang, she noticed more and more people coming up to the bandstand to listen. You couldn't call it a shake your booty song. Then more people came, all of them, it seemed, singing full throat.

Smack dab in the front stood Tina Ransom, who must have been in total culture shock from her surroundings. Maybe not, since she bellowed the lyrics as loudly as anyone. It made Cat consider the evidence. Tina had never married. Lately, it seemed as though she'd been loosening up, what with that spiffy semi-butch cut courtesy of Neil, and form-fitting jeans on a form well worth the denim.

Tina was always the highlight of Cat's trips to the library. Lingering near Tina in the stacks, she struck up conversations about books and movies. Cat enjoyed watching the way her face lit up.

Tonight, Tina was wrecking Cat's concentration. Who was she with tonight, or was she searching, and why did Cat even have an interest in the subject? And whoa, are we on the second go-round of the chorus or are we—yes, at the end. With the band finished, Cat kept the crowd singing a few more runs of "hush-hush" until everyone seemed satisfied.

Cracking his sticks, Jim immediately segued into the next number, an original Cat entitled "Illustrating the Night."

She's an artist, she's a painter, who's never been in vogue.
Attached to secrets she won't ever disclose.
She's a quarter-moon you see in a brand new light,

When she shines for you, illustrating the night.
She's her own best creation. Madeleine becomes Maria.
A fireball of wonders, oh, you can't wait to see her.
Who can touch the fire inside. A sparkle of her holy light.
And she shines, and she shines.
Count the colors in her palate, each feeling uncompromised.
You'll find a home when you fade into her eyes.
A portrait resting in the pale moonlight.
There's always a part of you illustrating the night.
She's her own best creation. Madeleine becomes Maria.
A fireball of wonders, oh, you can't wait to see her.
Who can touch the fire inside. A sparkle of her holy light.
And she shines, and she shines.
Upon her easel you're created. Oil and water, flesh and bone.
You live forever in a frame of gold, where you're never alone.

Now seated at a table with the band on break, Cat kept noticing how women walked by staring at her, how a beautiful drag queen resembling a harsher-edged Debbie Harry eyed them from the bar, and how Dani remained nowhere on the scene. Above the dance floor, a disco ball showered sparkles of light onto the dancers, colored tracers through the smoke and shadows.

The night had turned into a nonstop performance, where at the moment, she was playing the role of Neil's wife and the mother of his child. She wasn't still a clueless teen trying to fit in at a '70s gay bar, a kid trying to escape from under her father's thumb.

Neil returned to the table with a guest to further confuse her thinking. He booted Marco out of his chair to give Tina a seat by Cat. For years, she had admired Tina from afar or chatted her up at the library, but now, sitting next to her in a gay bar, Cat felt dumbstruck.

Neil handed Tina one of Cat's many margaritas—time to move on to some other concoction—then her dear, deadly husband piped up.

"Tina, you're looking so hot tonight. Really, guys, don't you think that is an amazing blouse?"

There were rumbles of agreement around the table. Tina was wearing a sheer chartreuse silk blouse over a white camisole. The shape of her breasts, hinted at, was exquisite.

"Do you want to dance?" Tina asked Cat.

Cat saw a surprised expression on Vonn's face, but the others had no reaction. Straight girls dance together all the time, even in a gay bar, right?

Cat heard Neil's voice cut through the pulsing beat. "Ladies, the invitation is to dance, not to sit."

Mimi left her seat and said to Neil, "I think it's time you and I shake our tail feathers, too."

The four of them traced intertwining lines as the music segued into Soul II Soul's "Back to Life," with Neil's moves often sending Cat closer to Tina or Mimi.

Time was running out on the break, and her husband again appeared to be trying to set her up with someone. Time was running out on the floorshow. She saw Dani, thought she saw Dani, walking out the door just as Tina was starting to dance a little closer.

Cat stopped moving in rhythm and walked over to the stage, knowing her band would follow. The show must go on, or more accurately, the show must return to the bandstand. Time to put some distance between her and Neil.

Chapter 7

Mandy had already read the police report, so all she needed was to gather some quotes from the staff to finish her article about the death of the hobo, Mr. McBride. Glancing at her watch, she had time to run by the library, then eat an early supper before the school board meeting began at seven.

It had already been a long enough Monday, one that began at the hospital's lab department, where she answered the questions in an interview for a change.

Marta Horton, the lab director, was a slim woman with piercing brown eyes. Mandy heard she was Filipino or Chinese, something like that, but she sounded pure Yankee. Mrs. Horton glanced at the application on her desk then fired both barrels.

"Why on earth would you come to work here? Patients don't just bleed, you know. They plaster you with vomit, pee, poop, and it doesn't matter how many gloves you put on during the day or even if you wear a mask, you won't escape. That's what happens around here, especially in ER. Stuff flies through the air, and you're in the middle of it."

Mrs. Horton paused. "You're still here."

"Ma'am, I haven't seen much compared to you. But, I've been through eight years of school board meetings, and I'm ready for a change."

"I'm not a ma'am, I'm a Marta," she said mirthlessly. "Do you need to give the boss man two or three weeks' notice?"

Mandy felt like road kill after that barrage. "Everyone who's quit at the paper gave two weeks. You're hiring me?"

"The light shines in her eyes." Marta jumped to her feet and grabbed a handled white tray of clear tubes and packaged syringes.

"Go by the business office. They'll have some forms for you to fill out, then they'll send you over to the clinic across the street so you can practice peeing into a bottle. First six weeks, you're a trainee, then after that, pay goes up. You catch on quick enough, we'll set you to running lab tests under supervision and even help send you to school. I'm sure Sherron told you that—she already gave you a good reference—then you come back in two weeks wearing a white lab jacket and, little girl, I'll show you the rest."

* * *

Mandy thought it was a good thing she'd quit smoking weed. Otherwise, she'd still be at the clinic trying to unclench her bladder instead of not meeting Miss Ransom's eyes during an interview.

They were sitting at a table hidden by the large-print section.

It figures. I'm trying to stay virtuous when the lady is starting to look much too interesting. It figures.

"Right here is where Mr. McBride spent most of his daylight hours reading books and magazines. He really wasn't much trouble."

This contradicted the previously voiced opinion of her helper, Otilia Garcia—Ricky's mother, Mandy realized—who didn't care for the man.

According to the police chief, relatives had yet to be located for McBride in his Pennsylvania hometown. Authorities there made it clear that disposing of his remains was not their problem, so he would sit in the funeral home's cold storage room for no more than ninety days.

George Bering, the library board president, told Mandy off the record he would make sure McBride received a proper burial.

To turn a police report into a human-interest piece required more detail than what people had given her so far. Mandy decided to ask about McBride's favorite authors.

"Political subjects. He'd pull out a book by George Will or a biography of Goldwater and be happy with that all day."

"What was he up to the rest of the time, I mean, when he wasn't here. Do you know?"

"I know he slept over by the benches next to the RV park, but a time or two in stormy weather, Father Guerra convinced him to stay with him. Sometimes, I—that is, people in town—would leave bags of food over by the RV park. One would say there was a measure of concern shown by our citizens, even if the object of their concern wasn't always as appreciative as one would hope."

Lord, it's only the librarian talking like a PBS documentary, so why am I so distracted? Send your angels to guard my doors and windows from all harm, and why do I have to be a constant spiritual warrior when I could just say to myself, *book lady has a nice bod*, and leave it at that? Why do I have to be so damned aware all the time? Excuse the language.

Miss Ransom had a small smile on her face. She must have been waiting for a question or some other sign of life.

"Sorry, it's been a long day." This time Mandy let her gaze linger. "I want to thank you for being helpful with articles over the years. You've always been patient with me."

"You've done a good job on your articles."

"Thanks, but I'm going to go to work at the hospital in a couple of weeks, so you'll be dealing with somebody new on the follow-up." Mandy kept her eyes on Miss Ransom, who didn't know that, at the moment, she was a battleground state in the war between heaven and hell.

"At the hospital? What department?"

"The lab. A friend of mine works there. Well, not in the lab, the business office. Sherron encouraged me to apply, and I'm glad I did."

Ms. Ransom's expression flickered into raw distress, then resumed its bland exterior, but Mandy caught it. "Sherron Steinhall?"

"You've met?"

"We're slightly acquainted."

Hilario might have the gaydar down, but Mandy didn't cover City Council meetings for eight years without picking up some understanding of nuance. *Slightly acquainted, my foot.* Book lady had a past.

* * *

Syd was sitting in front of the duplex in her Buick, the motor idling. Tina stepped out of her black Impala, and after a moment's hesitation, walked over to Syd. Call it progress, for Syd had made it to her block, even if she hadn't taken her key out of the ignition.

Syd rolled the window down and said tonelessly, "Get in."

She drove them over to the duck pond at Spencer Memorial Park, where they sat on a bench. Syd didn't seem disposed to talk.

The wind had picked up, rustling the tiny knot of brush and trees in the middle of the pond. Birds scattered to the sunbaked banks, squawking their discontent. In time, the pond, which had been established three years ago, would become a sanctuary. Not all things came in time.

"I don't want to see you anymore, Syd, if we're going to hide this completely. I've lied up 'til now, left out the truth in polite conversation so often that a few more lies are nothing, merely the price of living here, but I'm not made out of camouflage."

"We'll eat out more; in fact, are you hungry? We'll go over to Gardner's tonight."

Call it self-respect, or self-loathing, but Tina swore off being the other woman. Only now, she was entangled in a victimless affair.

Syd began rambling about how her day went at school. One of her senior honors English boys got into a fight in art class and had been suspended for a week. Before Syd went into detail, Tina interrupted.

"Listen."

"What?" Syd asked with a note of anguish.

"We need to talk about more intimate things. Something's been bothering me."

Syd's face shut down and a familiar wariness returned to her voice. "You don't want us to be friends anymore?"

Friends, she called it. Tina had no idea where to begin.

* * *

Cat spent Monday afternoon snaking the line to the dishwasher, clearing out an ungodly amount of gunk in order to make the machine operational again. That evening, she helped Wesley make sense of a complicated assignment in Sydney Melston's English class. Doing a modern-English translation of a complete act from *Hamlet* might daunt a college student, much less a high school freshman.

"She's real tough," Wesley said before his mother left his bedroom. "They say she used to be a lot of fun, but she don't act like it now."

"Doesn't. Doesn't act like it now."

"Yeah," he said.

"Do a few pages the way we worked the first two, then come get me."

Neil's eyes remained zeroed in on his *Vogue* magazine as she entered the bedroom and got undressed. She remembered the early months of their marriage when she couldn't change clothes in front of him, which reduced her to hiding in the closet or the bathroom. Pregnancy, delivery, and breastfeeding erased her modesty.

Now, wearing only panties and a black camisole she had pulled from the bottom drawer of her dresser, she asked Neil, "What do you think?"

"Looks nice," he said absentmindedly.

"Look up, Neil."

He did. "White would be better. More virginal."

"Like what Tina Ransom wore the other night."

He watched as she pulled off the camisole and slipped on a blue nightshirt. "You're darker than Tina, so white would stand out better."

"So, Tina or Mimi? Which one do you want me to go after?" She sat on the side of the bed and waited for a reaction.

The magazine dropped to his lap. "It's time."

"Are you wanting us to split up?"

"I've met someone."

All those trips to Dallas must have produced a contender. "You've been looking, I take it."

"No, but I found him anyway. I'm not leaving you, and I'm not going to make life hard on Wesley, but, yes, it's gotten more complicated."

"So you're pushing me to get busy on the dating scene to even things out."

"Think about it, Caterina. You getting into music, those lyrics you've been writing, all of that means something. You're so ready. It doesn't have to be someone from around here. If you want to take trips, people wouldn't think twice about it. They'd say, 'Cat's working on her career.' It's time, *mija*, it's time."

She slipped into bed and eased into her husband's arms. "Tell me about him."

"His name is Luis. He's younger than me. Hispanic."

"Big surprise. That's the only reason you banged me—that and you thought I was a drag queen."

"I thought you were a transsexual," he said in mock indignation. "It's obvious."

She popped him in the arm playfully.

"Bruiser. Okay, Luis works in real estate. He's originally from Borger, so he's a Panhandle boy."

"He been tested lately?"

"You know I wouldn't take a chance on that."

"How old is he?"

"Twenty-six. An old twenty-six. He's been on his own since he turned fifteen. Parents threw him out, so he moved in with his aunt in Dallas. He's applied at some realtor places in Lubbock, has interviews coming up."

"When were you planning to tell me?"

"I wasn't sure until now that he was going to schedule the interviews, and he'll be moving to Lubbock, not here," Neil said. "I'm not going to mess things up here, but I can't, I can't not have him in my life. You'll like him once you get to know him."

"Neil." She tried to forestall the worry in his face. "Neil, I want you to be happy. That's all I've ever wanted."

"That's all I've ever wanted for you."

"I know, but I'm not a kid anymore. You've helped me so far, but now I've got to find out what I want. It has to be me deciding, okay? Me."

They heard a knock on the door. "Mom?"

"On my way." Leaning over, she kissed her husband on the forehead.

"As our resident Shakespearean scholar," Neil said, "let me state for the record: to be or not to be, that is one hell of a question."

Chapter 8

"Ricky, what did you learn this week about allowing the Holy Spirit to work through you?" Brother Jesse asked.

Mandy checked on everyone's drink needs. No one needed a refill, then she tried to relax. Hilario made arrangements to be elsewhere during the prayer meeting. The new paint smell had faded, and ever since she steam-cleaned the carpet, their house had a cheery, if much too orange, atmosphere.

She had to give Ricky Garcia credit for toeing the party line.

He spoke through a split lip. "I learned that Joshua called me a fag not because he thought I really was one. He was mad because Julia was talking to me. And I shouldn't have kicked his ass—his butt. Sorry, Brother Jesse."

"That's okay, son. The Lord loves a hard worker. That's you, no denying. Y'all have to remember that Satan takes any situation and tries to bend it to his will." Brother Jesse addressed the rest of the group. "Ricky had the right idea in fighting back, spiritually, but he let Satan guide his anger. Y'all need to walk with the Holy Spirit if you want to be fulfilled as Christians. Friends, let's hold hands and pray our way home."

He beckoned them to stand and hold hands with one another.

Mandy said the correct phrases when her turn came around, but lost concentration during Ricky's stumbling effort. She opened her eyes to find Sherron gazing at her. Locked into each other, they listened to the men's voices saying amen, then everyone lifted their heads, the trance broken. They gradually worked their way to the door.

Sherron lingered after the others had left. "I had a good time," she said almost primly.

Mandy failed to suppress a laugh. "No, you didn't. You were bored silly."

"And you weren't?" Sherron marched into the kitchen, pulled a soft drink out of the fridge, and sat down at the table. "I swear,

Brother Jesse keeps saying the same things over and over, like they're supposed to help, but they don't. Ryan and me pray every night, and we've been slaving away at creating intimacy in the bedroom. I'm sick and tired of the whole thing."

She was not going to leave, evidently, so Mandy sat down beside her.

"It's not any of my business, but I thought you didn't have problems having sex with a man."

"Brother Jesse's been talking to Ryan, making him think it's partly his fault I'm not fulfilled, so Ryan is fulfilling me every chance he gets. I'm his sacred duty. Whoopee. It was more fun back when I thought I was doing something kind of twisted."

"Having sex with your husband, how's that twisted?"

"You know, doing something that's not really me, like I'm in a movie." She played with the pull-tab on her drink can. "I forgot. You've never been with a man. Scaredy-cat."

If the only way Sherron could have sex with her husband was by playing mind games, then she had never truly been with a man, either.

"I fooled around a bit in high school," Mandy admitted. "I couldn't get very far, but I did try. The one woman I was with, she said she enjoyed being with men. I don't think she had to pretend like you."

"Oh, Miss No Name again, or was she a Mrs.?" Sherron scooted her chair closer. "And you don't know, she might have been pretending with everybody."

Doris, despite her faults, never struck her as a liar. Mandy met Doris at the laundry while helping Momma wash quilts bequeathed them from Grandma Gabriel's attic. Doris stood in need of babysitting, as she had just started at the phone company, and her roughneck husband's schedule was too unpredictable. Mandy, who worked weekends at the funeral home, needed all the odd jobs she could scrounge for her college fund.

In retrospect, Doris may have had her in her sights from the beginning, because it only took two weeks before she drove Mandy out to the country, ending, coincidentally, at the Oliver caliche pit, in order to take care of the eighteen-year-old's lack of sexual experience.

Doris owned a few seams in her face from an outdoor life, yet with the lines came a youthful, naive nature that made it inevitable she would tell her husband what was going on between her and the babysitter.

This admission came at halftime of a Dallas Cowboys game. He drove over to the funeral home where Mandy was mopping the casket storage room. He screamed Doris's confession at her and promptly beat the crap out of her, which gave him plenty of time to drive home and catch the second half. She lay on that concrete floor alone for hours, bleeding and half-concussed, until her double vision cleared enough for her to make it home.

Momma had gone to bed by then, and her brothers were still out partying, so she was able to take a shower and go hide in her bedroom. No one questioned her explanation that she had the flu. No one cared except for Momma, who fixed her a bowl of potato soup the next day and placed a heating pad on her pillow.

Some time after that, she heard from a mutual acquaintance that Doris, her husband, and kids moved back to Odessa. Mandy didn't think Doris would ever try to contact her again, which turned out to be the case.

By then, Mandy was trying to get through freshman year at Texas Tech, but it all felt so pointless. The other kids' parents thought college was such a great idea that they provided steady emotional and financial support to their golden children. Those boys and girls, so comfortable joking around with each other—their lives weren't that easy, Mandy now suspected—still, their lives were based on planned optimism.

Mandy, on the other hand, was warned by her family that college would be a struggle and end in failure, so struggle she did, giving up after her first year, when a summer job at the newspaper turned into a lasting position. Her life then revolved around work and church, and if she ever yearned for emotional ties, there was a scar on her arm to remind her of the perils in such softheaded thinking.

So, the question of whether or not Doris thought of herself as being bisexual seemed beside the point to Mandy. Just like Doris, Sherron was married. How could it possibly turn out well?

Sherron sat across from her, wearing the same expression as earlier, demanding a response. This moment called for a passionate prayer, like the thousands Mandy had already delivered. Angels called for, demons banished.

She makes me feel alive. Angry, too, but alive. Send me to hell tomorrow, but for now, turn your eyes, Lord.

Sherron drew Mandy to her feet and led her to the living room sofa. In a rush, she kissed Mandy, her tongue too quick to explore.

"Slow down," Mandy murmured. She pushed down hands that were already busy trying to remove her blouse.

Mandy applied long, trailing kisses to Sherron's throat and cheeks, then with a quiet intensity, returned to her lips, working with unhurried care. A low sound not unlike a purr came from inside Sherron, who was no longer trying to force the pace. Mandy felt her rocking languidly underneath her.

Mandy broke away, leaning back against the sofa as she caught her breath.

Sweaty, with loose strands of hair in her face, Sherron no longer resembled the well-mannered wife who entered Mandy's house earlier in the evening.

"Why'd you stop?" she asked.

"Who were you just now?"

"Huh? Me, of course. Who'd you think?"

"You weren't pretending to be someone else?"

"No. What, what're you trying to say?" Sherron spoke with the bare hint of a stutter.

"Your life with Ryan may be nothing but a movie to you, but he thinks it's real."

Mandy wondered why she was committing sabotage when she had a willing and beautiful woman in her house. Who knew when that would happen again?

"I'm not going any farther with this until you figure out what's real to you," Mandy said.

Sherron started to speak then stopped. Tried again and stopped. She stood up and headed for the door, forgetting her purse, but Mandy hadn't forgotten.

Sherron tore her purse from Mandy's hands and said almost in a cry, "You're mean. I wish I hadn't come here tonight. You're just flat-out mean."

Mandy watched her walk out the door.

* * *

Syd sounded exhausted from a busy week at school, so Tina kept the call short. Syd had decided that since straight women shopped together, it should be a safe public activity for her and Tina. Did Tina want to go to Wal-Mart in the morning?

The few times they ventured out in public, Syd offered excuses to friends and acquaintances they encountered about why they were together, despite the lack of questions. Did anyone care that Syd was supposedly working on a school project with Tina's help. Didn't their friendship make enough of a cover story? Or was there even a friendship?

Tina told Syd she'd think about Wal-Mart.

Since she didn't feel up to cooking, she made a chicken sandwich, then sat out on her back porch. Becca happened to already be on her little square, slumped in a lawn chair and drinking a wine cooler.

It had been a while since they'd hung out together or even had much of a conversation, but Becca seemed so upset that Tina applied herself to the sandwich instead.

Becca lifted her head. "Hi," she said bleakly.

"Hi. Have you eaten? I have enough chicken to feed the block."

"No, I don't need anything." There was a long pause as Becca inspected her bottle.

"Okay," Tina said.

"You feel like walking?" Becca rose from her chair and took off.

Tina caught up to her as she rounded out the alley onto the street, the shadows around them sliding into dusk. A few minutes later, they passed by the neon-lit Sonic Drive-In, which was their traditional turnaround point. The wind began picking up, which made another good reason Tina had trimmed her hair. There were no bangs to lacerate her eyes.

"We can walk and talk at the same time, Becca. You know I'll listen."

Becca turned to face her. "I know you'll listen. I think you're one of the few people in this town who'd listen, but I can't talk about it. I just can't." She resumed her pace.

"I'm guessing here, but it's about your boyfriend in Lubbock, am I right?"

"My lover."

Boyfriend did seem a rather trite, high-schoolish phrase.

"Your lover. You've been spending a lot of time in Lubbock. Maybe he's wanting you to move up there?"

It was fortunate that Tina had built up her endurance by walking to work everyday. Otherwise, Becca's burst of speed would have left her far behind. Maybe Becca's lover was a Protestant, which would upset her family. Or maybe he was married.

"My lover's seeing someone else. Gracie saw them together. I'm the biggest idiot in the world. I've spent a ton of money on presents, acted like a fool, and for what? And for who?"

"You're sure he's cheating?"

"It's not the first time, so yes, I'm sure." Becca propelled them even faster down the street.

She took a turn that would get them back to the duplex. With her shiny black hair and strong, well-shaped nose, Becca resembled Tina's notion of Aztec royalty, but at the moment, her cheeks riven with tears, she looked a sodden mess. It was time to get her friend cleaned up.

Later, as they sipped on cups of coffee, Becca leaned back on the sofa and stared at the painting on the wall.

"I've been in here I don't know how many times and I've never asked. Who did that piece?"

"My mother." It was a near copy of a Van Gogh wheat field, but one of her better efforts. Mom somehow missed this piece when she destroyed her canvases during a bad spell. "I kept this one. My father has a couple of the other paintings."

"How is he doing?"

"Okay, I guess. We don't talk very often."

Tina planned to fly down to Houston over the Christmas holidays to see him and his wife, Ruby. She kept Tina up-to-date on Dad's activities, which currently included helping out on a Huntington's Disease newsletter and attending fundraisers. It was good that he kept busy.

Starting to look weepy again, Becca tried to rein herself in. "My parents and I, we talk all the time, but we don't say anything, not anything important."

"What would you tell them? Sorry, it's none of my business."

"I'd tell them I'm not who they think I am. I don't go to mass because I don't want to go to confession, because I can't tell Father Guerra I'm sleeping with someone."

The Ransom family had been faithful Methodists until the afternoon they buried Jack. Tina decided then that she and God didn't have anything to say to one another. On the whole, she tried to avoid spiritual discussions.

"It's not any of his business. It's between you and God. That's who you answer to, not your parents, not your priest, not even your church. I mean, love your family, but don't let them run your life."

Tina hoped that made sense, which perhaps it did because Becca tried for and achieved something close to a smile. That was a good thing, because she doubted Becca had any fluid left in her body to make more tears.

* * *

"I don't know if I'm feeling this one." Cat took another sip from her bottle of Corona.

"I think you sound fine."

Cat sat next to Mimi on her piano bench trying to follow the melody line on the sheet music. Mimi thought they could pick up some pocket money playing piano bars and coffee houses together, splitting the take fifty-fifty instead of with a full band. It wouldn't be a bad idea if Mimi could hook up with an actual jazz singer. Mimi said she didn't like singing leads, for some reason.

"I can't make the notes sustain the way they need to," Cat said.

"You don't have to hold a note forever, just smooth it out a bit when you quit." Mimi demonstrated by singing a bar from the song. "Nancy Wilson, Dinah Washington, they're good ways to approach it. And, you know, Lady Day sort of did the same thing when drinking and drugging made her all crack-voice hoochie mama. She couldn't keep the flow, so she had to go with attitude and placement."

"So I'm a crack-voice hoochie mama?" Cat said with a laugh. "You're free with the compliments."

"You know what I mean. And Neil thinks you can sing this style of music."

Neil probably suggested the duo idea to Mimi and did, in fact, call Mimi to set up the rehearsal.

"Not everything in my life has to be routed through Neil. He's not my father." Cat shut off her rant.

Mimi raised her eyebrows but said nothing.

"Neil and I... I don't know what to call it, what we have. A personal arrangement."

"An open marriage?"

"In a way. No, because open means something else, I think, where they're with each other, and they're also seeing other people. That's not what Neil and I have."

She frowned. Their parents knew, as did Neil and Cat's siblings, but no one discussed it. For the first time, Cat was discussing her marriage with an outsider. She discovered she lacked the proper words, the vocabulary to describe the situation. Why was she making this effort? Because Mimi needed to know. And why did Cat think that?

"Let me take a shot at it. You and Neil, you're not intimate, but he dates men sometimes, and you, you date other people."

"Not yet. I don't date other people."

"But you're thinking about it."

"Yeah." Cat wondered why she couldn't make the move that Neil wanted her to make and, for all she knew, Mimi expected. She liked Mimi, thought she was attractive, but something kept shutting her down.

Smiling, Mimi closed the sheet music then opened a different copy. With a relaxed air, as though they'd been discussing the weather, she began talking about "I Cover the Waterfront."

"Let's drop the verse and go straight to the chorus, then we can segue into the Sarah Vaughan number. People don't remember verses on the old songs, anyway."

"Mimi?"

"What's that?"

"Thanks."

"Sure thing. Now, this is the intro."

Chapter 9

Hilario could have said a lot of things on the way into Lubbock about Mandy's catch and release last night. Hadn't he already told her that closeted femmes were nothing but trouble?

That morning, she called Brother Jesse to inform him she was dropping out of the prayer circle. He told her Sherron beat her to the draw, claiming Mandy made her uncomfortable.

She felt so calm while talking to Brother Jesse, as though she had announced, "Yes, I've decided to go to hell. I hear the music's great." That named, implacable dread had disappeared. Yesterday God was out to destroy her, and today she felt like a spool of thread unwound in Momma's sewing basket. More than that, she didn't know.

Instead of offering advice, Hilario sang along to his tape of Emmylou Harris's "Two More Bottles of Wine."

"Since when do you listen to country?" Mandy asked when the song ended.

"Thomas is a very, very bad influence. I'm thinking of buying a cowboy hat."

"I wish you could have talked him into coming with us."

"Dream on, *prima*. He's a queer vampire, only comes out in the shadows, and besides, he's been running the module builder all week. Hey, hey, I got it. You could go out with him. Since he split up with that teacher, he's been needing someone. You could do it."

"Why did he split up with Melston? She give him a failing grade?"

"I don't know. He won't say. It's like the third time they've broken up. I think it's 'cause she doesn't want to get married, and he's worried people are talking about her."

Mandy hadn't considered the possibility Sydney Melston might be gay.

"And people wouldn't talk about Tommy and me? Dream on."

"No one knows you're gay, and if you wore a little makeup, you know, tried? You could wear the ring, let Thomas pay your bills, and solve both our problems."

Mandy thought it was enough of a step that she was about to enter a gay bar for the first time in her life, yet Hilario couldn't resist making elaborate plans for their future. In his own way, Hilario was a cockeyed romantic.

By way of Mary Eckert's need for a paint job on her property, some extra money had entered Hilario's pockets, and as for his love life, the new watch on his wrist proved that Tommy had upped his level of gifting.

"If we got married, Tommy would be telling the whole town he's gay, and just because people don't yell faggot in my face doesn't mean they're ignorant, at least, not in that way. Maybe they have some couth about them."

When they walked in the door, Hilario immediately took them to the bar to place their orders. She hadn't known what to expect. It looked like any another club, until she saw two women on the dance floor working an intricate two-step move that involved twirl reverses from one another, then rejoining at the hip to spin as a unit. Mandy didn't think she could map it out, let alone dance it. She had never seen women dance together as a serious couple, not just killing time while waiting for a man to come along.

A lanky woman in western wear waited for her turn to order. Looking up at her, Mandy realized she could stare all she wanted and nothing would happen, other than maybe a verbal slapdown.

How would Sherron react to such a place? She probably would assume she'd rule the roost, but in fact, there were several attractive femmes in the bar, meaning that the available pool of lesbians was much larger than Mandy thought. She laughed for no particular reason, causing the cowgirl to let out a laugh of her own.

"What's funny?"

"It's my first time in a gay bar, and I guess it's not funny. It's just that it's all new to me."

She looked a few years older than Mandy, with a craggy, handsome face as though she really were a cowgirl. She dressed like a resident of Marlboro Country and was taller than Mandy, but then, so was everybody. Finding an open barstool, the woman sat down beside her, instantly reducing the size factor.

"Dani," she said, offering a hand. "You might call me the welcome wagon."

Tina hadn't been sitting long at her table when she saw Mandy Gabriel walk in the door.

Tina knew she had an excuse for the night of Cat Acuff's soul- and body-stirring performance. She couldn't have been the only plausible straight in the club that night, setting aside her bizarre quasi-dancing with Cat. On a no-show night, why on earth would Tantona's librarian be at a gay club?

As for Mandy, there without Sherron, Tina figured this was a scoop the former reporter would keep to herself. It occurred to Tina that she could go roust Syd out of bed and be satisfied with what scraps of emotion came her way.

No. For better and quite possibly for worse, she had decided to spend the evening sipping on a wine spritzer and studying her peers.

What was going on with her? She had a quasi-girlfriend, a job, a savings account, and an apartment, all in Tantona. There was no reason to risk her future, except that she might be dying.

Wine wasn't cutting it, not tonight.

Back at her seat, Tina contemplated a pitcher of beer and her empty mug. The fog, unsteadiness, and restlessness she'd been experiencing could be nothing more than stress. There could be an innocent explanation, for someone other than her.

Her mother denied she was sick for several months after she began showing symptoms, for she was too busy handling Jack's pre-ordained death spiral.

Tina lacked that distraction. Mom's father had Huntington's, Mom had Huntington's, Jack had Huntington's, and if Tina possessed the gene, just like them, she would die of it. The logic was inescapable. A doctor would say they died of complications rather than the disease, which Tina believed to be a distinction without a difference.

When her mother was Tina's current age of forty-three, she started walking around during meals, restless and confused. Then came the clumsiness, tics, depression, falls, and rages. I'll be damned if I'll wait on Syd to get serious, for I may be damned already, she thought. Well, well, here comes Mandy Gabriel with Ms. Wrangler.

To her credit, Mandy didn't pull a "gotcha." Instead she claimed it was her first night at the club, then introduced her new acquaintance, a woman named Dani.

"Where's Sherron?"

Mandy blinked several times. "Where do you think?"

"She's sleeping with the hubby?"

"You got that right. I don't expect you to believe this, but I sent her home last night with a kiss. Okay, a lot of kisses, but just that, and I don't intend to see her anymore." She sat down across from Tina as Dani pulled over a chair to join them.

"Who's Sherron?" Dani asked, eyeing the pitcher.

"Dani, you're welcome to get a glass from the bartender. I'll need some help drinking this down. Sherron? Sherron is the biggest lesbian in Tantona, Texas."

"Sounds like a handful." Dani managed to get the waiter's attention.

Two more mugs arrived as Mandy and Tina swapped war stories, then three women, friends of Dani's, dragged a table over to stretch the seating.

By the time another pitcher of beer shrank to half-empty and two more women joined the table, Tina discovered that Mandy had been telling the truth about it being her first time in a gay club, and that it would be wise to stay a while. She didn't think she drank more than her share of the beer, but given that the walls were starting to move, she must have exceeded her alcohol limit by a factor of ten.

While the others were up and dancing to a song by Cher, Dani sat nearby and asked Tina what she knew about cats.

"Please, not a librarian question."

Dani leaned back in her chair and laughed. "A woman named Caterina, not the little creatures of the night, my dear. Cat Acuff. She lives in Tantona. She's been singing lately."

"Oh God, yes, she's been singing. If you're not gay before you hear her sing, you will be by the time she's through." Tina felt sure she was bubbling, not to mention babbling, and while she strove for a socially redeemable personality—not inclined to flower walls at parties—no one would ever claim she oozed effervescence.

It turned out that Dani and Cat were former best friends back in their high school days. After performing complex calculations involving Cat's gay husband, Dani's butchness, and Tina's wishful thinking, she could well believe that Dani and Cat had a sexual history. Maybe that was why Cat never mentioned a husband in all their library talks. Such a striking woman, Cat. Tina needed another haircut, and soon.

Along about her third dance with Dani, she had begun to notice the rangy woman's habit of slow dancing even on the fast ones. Tina broke away to the restroom just in time to unload the contents of her roiling stomach as well as her toenails and a kitchen sink imported for the occasion.

Afterward, she saw a pop art painting on the wall of two women kissing, the long tendrils of their hair scant coverage for their skin. As art, she considered it crap. As erotica, it might be effective, although at the moment she didn't feel anything. That, she suspected, had been the point of getting drunk.

It was then she realized that Mandy had been helping her during the throw-up and was currently applying a moistened paper towel to Tina's face. Looking down, she saw herself on a rickety folding chair next to the trashcan.

"Do you think you're through?" Mandy asked.

She questioned her stomach. "I think so."

"Dani and her friends are planning on going over to IHOP. Hilario and I talked it over, and I'm going to drive you home. You shouldn't be behind the wheel."

"Where's Dani?"

"She kept topping off your beer. Maybe you should think about why she did that."

"Maybe she wanted to unwind. Me, unwind." Tina tried to untangle her tongue. "How short are you?"

Mandy smiled. "Five-foot-two-and-a-half. How old are you?"

"Five-foot-six. Oh. Forty-three. I don't usually this much. Drink. Much."

"That's obvious."

Tina swore she felt better as Mandy and Hilario walked her to her car, and she did, honestly, but her feet weren't working very well. Tucked into the passenger seat, she gaped at the chain-link glow of highway lights as Mandy tooled them back home. She wondered why the reporter, make that junior lab tech or whatever she did now, didn't seem to have any nerves in her whatsoever.

"Why is that?" she asked.

"Why is what?"

Drifting off, she woke up in her driveway as Mandy was opening her door.

"Okay, you need to help me on this," Mandy said with a grunt, placing Tina's feet on the ground.

Ow. Holding her head where she bumped it into the car door, Tina vowed to never get this drunk again. She might well be a freaking vegetable this time next year, but she planned to hang onto every last brain cell until forced to blow them out.

"You have a gun?" Mandy asked as she took off Tina's shoes. Somehow they'd made it inside her apartment. Farther than that, to her bed, and she must have been thinking aloud.

"No, I don't have a gun, and I'm not suicidal."

"You don't sound life-affirming, I can tell you that." She removed Tina's sweat-soaked jeans. "Listen. You don't know that you have the Woody Guthrie thing, but you are going to die. We all are."

"That's your idea of talking me off the ledge? It's a good thing you didn't go into police work."

She must have yapped about everything on the way home, making it safe to assume that Syd got outed in the process.

"I'm just saying that if your brain does go bad, you'll have a little time to decide what to do, but I wouldn't use a gun, if I were you."

Odd. This woman had just now undressed her, tucked her under percale, and even fetched a glass of iced tea to place beside the bed, yet Tina did not feel embarrassed over being nude and drunk in front of her.

"Why not a gun?"

"Eight years of police reports. You try for suicide, but the bullet goes somewhere else. You don't want to know what that looks like. Pills you'll puke up, then there's throwing yourself under the train. Very Madame Bovary, but forget it. The train goes too slow through this area. You might only lose your legs. Slice your wrists? Well, that could work, but your survival instinct kicks in, not to mention the clotting factor, and the same goes for drowning, if you could find a body of water around here that's deep enough. You say you want to die, you try to die, but your body thinks it's a bad idea."

"What works?" Tina couldn't help but ask. The tea tasted strong and unsweetened, the way she liked it.

Mandy shook her head. "Do your own research. I'm not helping."

"My breath must be awful."

"It shouldn't be. I fed you breath mints on the way home. I'm just glad you didn't choke on them."

"You didn't mention that as a suicide option." Mandy drove, which meant her rescuer had no easy way of getting home at such a late hour. "You're staying."

"Excuse me? Oh, that's okay, I can—"

"No, really. You're staying. You can sleep in here or you can sleep on the sofa. Either way you stay. I'll drive you home in the morning."

"Later this morning."

"Whatever. Whenever."

* * *

Cat reluctantly put down the massive rib she had been gnawing on and followed Marta Horton down the hallway.

It had been a fun barbecue thus far, with everybody contentedly working his or her way through the most talented parts of a cow.

The Hortons, while no longer imbibers, allowed the thirsty to bring their favorite social lubricants. This had to be a policy unpopular with their new church peers, as no doubt the dancing would be, when it broke out on the patio. Cat could see why the Hortons converted en masse, given Felix's now-halted slide into alcoholism, but it seemed to her that Kendra, their high school sophomore daughter, could have used a few more dunks in the baptistry.

"So, what's this about Kendra?"

Marta's eyes glinted with sharp-edged humor, or at least Cat thought it was humor. "Make that Kendra and Wesley."

"Good Lord."

"Yes, your boy's fallen for an older woman. Or, in this case, that flighty daughter of mine. I don't know how she got into this family. The others are little sweethearts, but Kendra, hmph. I knew once she discovered boys, she'd never go back to Barbie, but lately, Felix and I both have to make sure she's where she says she's at, even secretly reading her diary, and now she's dragged Wesley into her lair. They haven't done the deed yet, but we need to consider a trial separation."

"That sounds like a good idea." Cat tried to appear sympathetic but rejoiced that her son wouldn't have to deal with the double whammy of being gay with gay parents.

Marta looked at her curiously. "You are the most positive person I know. Smiling like that. Me, I want to put a lock on Kendra's door and not let her out 'til she turns eighteen."

"Oh, believe me, I'm concerned, and I will be talking to Wesley tomorrow."

Not tonight. He and Kale would be in the middle of an epic Nintendo battle. Let the boys practice at being men that way.

Cat went back to the party, where Felix, robust and hairy with strong lungs, was positioning his stereo speakers for perfect play on the patio, getting some good-natured harassment from Neil. Ryan Steinhall stood nearby. She had never seen Ryan at the Horton parties before, as he usually drew the line at alcohol events, but she knew him from their forays in the library a couple of years ago.

She had been working her way through a passion for the likes of Amado and Tanizaki that prompted her to bug Tina about interlibrary loan shipments. Cat kept coming across Ryan in the stacks, or else he'd be sitting out in his pickup, talking on a mobile phone.

Ryan, always crisply turned out in a polo shirt and dark slacks, could not stay away from the library, so they got to talking, doing what readers do, trying to convert others to their genre, but while Cat enjoyed Elmore Leonard, Ryan didn't care for *Tent of Miracles* or *The Makioka Sisters*.

Did others notice their bookish ways, or think an affair was going on? It said something about her mindset that she never considered how it might look to others. Ryan seemed unhappy then, going so far as to mention being put out with his wife, yet he never made a play for Cat. Since then, he sometimes dropped by the shop for a haircut, and if Cat happened to be there, they discussed authors.

Tonight, something about him seemed off, but the source of his discomfort appeared obvious.

Sherron had decided to attend the barbecue wearing expensive-looking jewelry, black spandex leggings, spiked heels, and a slinky, gold lamé top. Cat, like the other women, dressed more casually—tonight in jeans and a Texas Tech top—but she didn't feel challenged by the fashion throw-down.

Ryan, unshaven and unsteady, ignored his wife and quick-stepped to Cat's side.

"So, how's it going, Cat? I've been hearing all kinds of wonderful things about your singing career."

"Thanks, but I'm kind of glad my career is on hold for the weekend. We've been rehearsing or playing gigs every weekend for a while now. That Neil, he's so good at managing us, I don't know if I'm coming or going."

Ryan laughed too loud and too long in response, making Cat wish she'd not relied on a cliché. What was up with him?

He led her by the arm into the backyard, well behind the barbecue pit. Glancing back toward the patio as they walked, Cat saw Neil looking at them, curious but not intervening. She had the strong suspicion Ryan didn't want to swap books tonight.

"You and I, we understand each other, you know?" Ryan said.

He stood in the shadowy alley side of the Horton's oak tree, forcing Cat to move closer to hear him.

"Ryan, we haven't talked in a while. I don't know that we've ever really—"

"We have the same problem. I can't think of anything else to try, I can't fix her, and Brother Jesse keeps telling me what's right. And I see you, you've been dealing with it longer than I have. There you are, with a son. He's older than Emily, so you know, you know how to handle it."

If she touched him right now, the man would jump a mile. In a calm, even voice, she said a few soothing words intended to slow his pace, which was beginning to speed up physically as well as emotionally.

He walked to the alley gate, started to work the latch, and then turned around, distressed. "I can't look at her right now."

"We live less than three blocks away. Let me tell Neil we're going over."

Cat decided to keep him in the kitchen, well away from soft cushions and dim lighting, just in case he developed certain notions. She brewed them coffee, then offered Ryan a slice of Sarah Lee chocolate cake. He accepted, although he ignored the plate, but the coffee went down at a throat-searing rate as he explained how his visits to the library had been about keeping track of a woman he thought his wife was seeing.

"It doesn't matter who it was," he said.

She had to be Tina Ransom, as the only other competitor in looks there, Mary Eckert, would have laughed Sherron out of the building. With a start, Cat realized she felt intensely jealous of Sherron.

"Out of the blue, Sherron decided we should start hosting library board meetings and fundraisers at the house. She never even had an interest in the library until she laid eyes on... that woman."

"I imagine it was Tina. I won't tell anyone."

At that small kindness, he slumped over in his chair, hands on his face, trying to contain his emotions. After a while, he lifted his head, took out his neatly pressed handkerchief, and wiped his face.

"I should go. I don't want the rest of the party to think I'm doing something I shouldn't over here. You've been very nice to me."

"Don't leave until you're ready." Cat thought the man took good manners to the extreme. "Neil trusts me, and his trust is well-earned."

"That's just it." Ryan exploded. "You're married to a faggot. It's obvious what he is, but you don't care, and that's obvious, too. I've seen the two of you at football games, seen you everywhere, and you're arm-in-arm, crazy about each other. You love him."

Did she want to even try to explain? She could stumble through her words with Mimi, who was sympathetic in her own mysterious way, but to talk to an upset heterosexual man who could end up blabbing the truth all over town?

There he was, wounded to the core and thinking Cat possessed a magical approach to living with a gay person that could salvage his own marriage. If she had to, she could lie about it later if the story got out.

"I'm gay, too," she said. Ryan looked stunned. "I haven't been with anyone since before we got married, but I'm gay."

"You're sure?" The note of yearning in his words startled her.

"I'm positive. Some men are beautiful to look at, and some are friends, like my husband, who is both, but if I give my heart to someone, it will be to a woman."

"If you want my advice," Ryan said, "don't even think about Sherron. She came home last night from the prayer circle crying her eyes out and wouldn't tell me what was wrong, but I kept after her until she owned up. I knew she'd chase after Mandy Gabriel, and if that dyke had any sense, she'd send Sherron packing, which she did. A prayer circle for queers—what a big, fat waste of time."

That was a lot to digest over her slice of chocolate heroin. Mandy Gabriel, whose parents owned the shop next door to the salon. A prayer circle for local gays, which meant that there were enough in town, or at least in Ryan's church, to make it viable.

"Leave Sherron. It's one thing to put up with it if you're gay yourself, but you're not, and it's even bearable if you're straight with a quote-unquote arrangement, but this, this isn't working, Ryan. You said it yourself. You can't fix her. You're making each other miserable, and is that putting a smile on God's face? I don't see how."

She instantly regretted her words. Marital advice and spiritual commentary. Why stop at that? Tell the man how to raise his child, Oprah.

The door from the garage opened, and her husband and son walked in. Wesley eyed the cake with palpable longing, seeming not to notice that his mother was sitting with Ryan. Neil had a harder look in his eyes. Her guest made a faltering getaway.

It was late, but not that late, and since Wesley probably spent more time tonight playing than eating, she gifted him with the untouched slice. Gratified, her son retreated to his bedroom, leaving the third member of the Acuff family seated at the table, pretending to ignore the cake.

"While you were having a little chat with Ryan, I was playing Father Confessor to half the people at the party. Gods, woman, don't leave me stuck with Felix again."

"He's back to drinking?"

"I wish. Don't look at me that way. And yes, I know, you were doing the same thing, fixing whatever's wrong with Ken Doll the Bookworm, but I do get tired of us being relationship fairies to half our crowd."

"It's because we can't talk about ourselves, not really, so they think we're perfect." She poured him a cup of coffee and refilled her own.

"And we're not?"

Neil popped a bite of cake into his mouth, dropping stray crumbs on his Texas Tech T-shirt.

"Of course we are, dear. And what's the matter with Felix?" She leaned over to brush his shirt.

"It's hard to translate what he says sometimes because it's mixed in with the tool-talk and baseball stats and now sermonettes from the Good Book, but what I'm getting is that he hates Brother Jesse, but Marta's afraid to try another church because she thinks Felix won't stay dry unless he's getting his chestnuts toasted every Sunday. Oh, and let me tell you about that Steinhall woman."

"I already know. Ryan told me she's a lesbian."

After starting a fresh pot, she turned to look at her husband, who had a surprised look on his face. "I'm guessing that's not what you were about to tell me."

"Nooo, although it would explain why she came on to me by the bathroom, not more than three feet from Marta. I'd say Sherron wanted a witness for her heterosexual rampage. She also made a pass at LaSonda's husband, which is a suicidal gesture. Now, what's this about you and Ryan, not to mention the lesbian, and spare none of the details, please. I feel like being an outraged husband tonight."

Chapter 10

Mandy couldn't believe she ever thought Tina had an ounce of retreat in her, and not simply because of her performance at the bar. Given the pressures in her life, Tina was overdue for a meltdown.

The first evidence of backbone came over breakfast. Just a simple apology, then "you want more eggs?" Tina said over breakfast that she was the first in her family that she knew of to finish college, which she probably said to put Mandy at ease. Mandy didn't need the advisory. She saw that away from the library, Tina had a more casual attitude.

After the eggs, a perfect over-easy, Tina took her home, where Mandy changed into shorts. Almost without discussion, they decided to spend the afternoon together.

Now they were sitting in Tina's car, Sonic drinks in hand, gazing at the one truly scenic spot in the county.

To get there, one started with a twelve-mile drive down a tarmac farm-to-market road south of town, then two miles farther on a dirt road. Travelers came up over a sizeable hill, itself a novelty, then the road dipped sharply next to Chaco Draw, which had been a going stream when the earliest non-Natives first came through in the late 1890s.

Long since turned into tangled brush, it showed signs of its former life along about September in a wet spell, allowing visitors to walk along the banks and pretend to see a raging torrent in the spare rivulets. About half a mile farther a rogue outlier of the Caprock rose, pushing jagged rocks from a plateau start-up that God halfheartedly began, then abandoned.

Tina struck her as lacking in pioneer, not to mention hiking, spirit, so Mandy decided not to suggest they leave the car. Instead, they sat there with the windows rolled down and talked about people in town, the bar from last night, and other women.

"I guess I should leave her." Tina spoke tentatively.

"You were never with Syd in the first place."

From the way Tina reacted, Mandy realized she'd overstepped a boundary. She might as well keep going. "If she were a man, would you still say you've made any kind of commitment, that you're involved with each other?"

"In a way. I guess."

A high, thin crease formed on Tina's forehead as she pondered the concept. Mandy thought those few age lines on her face were interesting. Sherron would spend time covering it with makeup, but Tina didn't seem to care. Her lack of concern may have come from expecting an early death.

The crease disappeared. "No. If she was a man and I was straight, I wouldn't have called her back after that night. Oh. I assume I told you about how she took charge, how I didn't get to do... that."

"The subject came up."

Yeah, it had come up a few times, mixed in with speculation about Cat Acuff. Mandy had to admit the hairdresser's wife sounded gay, according to the otherwise unreliable Dani. Also during the drive, Tina frequently voiced her fears about going insane. Mandy couldn't claim any medical expertise after a few days working at the hospital, but it seemed to her that Tina had cause to worry.

She had reason to curl into a ball, yet she sat next to Mandy humming along to a Madness tape. Maybe the band name was what attracted Tina to them.

Stopping in mid-note, Tina turned her face to Mandy. "I'm forty-three."

"Fifteen years older, thereabouts. I'm not going to get any taller."

"As if that matters."

"And what's fifteen years? Look, let's give us time. After all, we hardly know anything about each other. I did learn a lot about you from last night."

"I know you read Stephen King, but you don't care for Anne Rice, which I think is a point in your favor. You like to read about travel. And I don't think you even like Rita Mae Brown's books, but you check them out."

"Sometimes you have to take one for the team." *Does she have every patron's habits memorized?*

Maybe she was going through a bad patch last night, Mandy thought. Smiles passed between them, then almost casually, Tina leaned over and kissed her. It was a little peck. The second kiss took much longer.

* * *

"Greetings and salutations," Becca said when Tina opened her back door. "You want to join us out here? We have beer in the fridge, and Gracie brought some barbecue from Stubbs."

Who could refuse that invitation? Since her arrival home, Tina had checked her answering machine: three hang-ups and Syd's terse "pick up the phone." She needed to call Syd and deliver the *coup de grace*, but for the moment, Syd could wait.

Gracie Munoz, a Lubbockite originally from Tantona, was a sweet-faced woman around Becca's age of mid-forties. She wore a pair of short-shorts and a halter top that Tina supposed were meant to be age-defying. Then again, Tina used to dress like an old woman, so she had little room to judge others' fashion choices.

As she worked down a plate of brisket, Tina listened to Gracie mince words about Becca's ex. Gracie seemed several times on the verge of letting loose her tongue but then would shut up.

"I know I shouldn't go over there tonight, so I'm not," Becca said. "I have to work tomorrow, remember? You don't have to tell me, I know what to do, but would you answer the phone this next time, okay?"

Becca looked at Tina as though she expected her friend to add something to the conversation.

"I'm with Gracie on this. Be strong. Don't let the man sweet-talk you into coming back to him. He's not worth it."

Gracie shot an irate look at Tina. "I'm going to get another beer." She clacked her heels up the steps.

"You haven't talked to him again, have you?"

Becca took a bite of potato salad, chewed slowly, then set her plate down and sat back in her chair. "We need to talk, you and I. And once you know what's going on, I'll understand if you don't want to be friends anymore, or if you end up moving. It's been nice having you as a neighbor all this time, but I won't hold a grudge."

"Becca, we've known each other forever. When I decided to go run the library and everyone told me I was crazy to take the pay cut, you were one of the few people who supported me. There's nothing you can tell me that would change my opinion of you."

And if you'd seen how I acted last night, you'd have to go a long way to top that.

"My lover—my ex-lover—goes by B.D., which is short for Bertha Duarte," Becca said hesitantly. "A *jota, lesbiana*, a real dyke, although she doesn't look it quite so much now that she's let her hair grow out some."

Tina was floored by the news, and then chagrined. Hadn't Becca practically put it on a billboard for her to figure out?

"I'm sorry I hadn't told you the truth, but I didn't want to upset you or make you think you had to worry about me behaving improperly."

"No, Becca, this changes nothing for me. You're my friend."

Tina couldn't say the obvious thing, she couldn't. Even though Tina had no intention of ever going out with Syd again, still, Becca might see the connection. Syd made her promise—enough. Enough.

"Becca, I'm a lesbian."

A can of beer fell to the concrete behind her. Gracie could unbite her tongue now.

Becca stared at her. "Are you sure? You're not just saying that?"

"I kissed a woman about an hour ago."

And she would have done a lot more if Mandy hadn't been the sensible one. Let's wait and do it properly when we know each other better, Mandy said, but all Tina could think, if one could call it thinking, was that here existed a woman who didn't seem afraid. That proved more than enough to trigger a major attack of libido.

"Becca, I haven't had a lot of experience, but I know what I am. I just wish I'd figured out you were a lesbian long before now, so you wouldn't have felt so alone dealing with B.D."

Becca's phone rang and then, as though setting off a reaction, so did Tina's. They looked at each other and shook their heads.

"Do you want me to answer?" Gracie asked.

"No," Becca and Tina said simultaneously.

* * *

Mimi and Cat were in their fourth rehearsal as a jazz duo, and they were beginning to figure out what numbers worked for them.

Once Cat got going, she could manage in jazz, and on "Between the Devil and the Deep Blue Sea," she even improvised some vocal riffs over Mimi's playing, causing her accompanist to flash a rare full-fledged smile.

How on earth could Cat ask this woman out, when she didn't know whether or not Mimi was gay, Cat happened to be married, and, by the way, wasn't this her band, so wouldn't Mimi feel pressured?

Or maybe it boiled down to the fact that, although she liked Mimi, her feelings went no deeper than that. She could no more fall in love with Mimi than she could with Marta Horton, despite Neil's cheerleading. He seemed to think that any attractive, ambiguous adult female crossing her path could be fair game.

Cat, the feline predator, stalking her prey. She grinned at this description—as if she had an ounce of aggression in her bones—and continued putting away the microphone.

"What are you thinking?" Mimi asked.

"Oh, nothing. You don't want to know."

The phone in the salon rang, and since the place was closed, it was probably Neil. She stepped out to the register and took the call. Neil sounded worried, but still insouciant.

"You haven't seen either of the Steinhalls, have you?"

"No."

"Sherron called a while ago, wanting to talk to you. I said you were rehearsing, and she said I ought to keep my wife at home. In fact, she said we should keep our nose out of her business. Apparently, you and I only have one nose between us."

"It's my nose today."

"Of course. Anyhow, the little dear completely forgot to come on to me, so I suppose I've been rejected." He turned more serious. "Do what you want, but I'd think hard before talking any more to Ryan, at least until the two of them get their problems worked out."

That was sound advice she intended to follow, but those two weren't going to get their problems worked out. She hung up the phone. Looking through the plate glass, she saw a late-model, gold Town Car pull up to the curb. Sherron got out and came up to the door.

"You want me to stay?" Mimi said with a please-don't-get-me-involved sound to her voice.

"No, go on."

Moments later, Mimi had sped off the lot, and Sherron was doing a Ryan-worthy pace through the shop. Cat decided to go with firm over friendly.

"If you're looking for Ryan, he's not here, and he won't be anywhere I'm at. I have no interest in him."

Sherron stopped in her tracks. "Don't get me started. I know Ryan's not here. He's staying over at his sister's house, and he took Emily with him. He said if I contested, he'd tell everyone what kind of woman I am. I'd never see my baby again. I could screw the judge on the courthouse lawn today, and no one would believe it was real."

"Because it wouldn't be real."

What was it about the Steinhalls? Cat couldn't keep her mouth shut. Not in trophy wife mode today, Sherron did have on matching shorts and blouse, but with her skin scrubbed clean and her hair barely touched by a brush, there was a wildness to her, a vulnerability not visible the night before.

"How'd you like it if I told on you, huh?" Sherron fired back.

Ryan, that idiot.

"He kept saying he didn't do anything with you. Bull, I said. Then he said, 'You know she's not getting any from that husband of hers.' So he told me. He told me about you, and then he left. He'd taken Emily to church and come back so he could pack some of her things while I was in the shower. When I got out, he was about to leave. He didn't want to talk. He said he'd done all the talking he felt like doing, which was to you last night. Happy now? He took my baby, he took my Emmy, and I can't do a thing about it."

The agitation in her voice escalated, then something in her collapsed. She slumped into a chair. Taking one slow, beleaguered spin, she stared into the mirrored wall.

"I didn't talk to him about your daughter. I'm sorry, I'm sorry he did that to you. I didn't know he had that in mind."

She barely knew Sherron, didn't know Ryan all that well, and yet somehow she'd gotten sucked into their drama. *The party.* It came to her. Ryan went there looking for Cat, desperate for a solution, regardless of what she said to him, and the fact that she came out to him mattered little. It only meant that an affair was out of the question.

"It seems to me that Ryan must have been planning this for a while, before he ever talked to me. Thinking about it, anyway." Cat sat down in the chair beside Sherron.

The silence dragged into a long moment. "We have a fridge in back. Would you like a Dr. Pepper?" Cat asked.

"Do you have something stronger?" Sherron asked in a mumble.

Cat sipped on her bottle of Samuel Adams as Sherron first plunked on the drums then produced a credible keyboard version of "Lean on Me." Sherron seemed to feel somewhat better, although she had barely touched her bottle.

"I can sing, too. Not like you, but I've been doing solos at church."

"When did you hear me sing?"

"During the Pioneer Celebration a few years ago. Ryan's big in Rotary. We had a cotton candy booth on the square. You were singing with that country band. I thought you sounded really good."

"Thanks."

"You know, Ryan's sister and I are thinking about running my daughter for Pioneer Queen when she gets a little older." Defiantly, Sherron wiped away the tears. "I never did anything improper around my child. I always conducted myself like a lady. Ryan made it sound like I was going to bring bull dykes through my back door, like I didn't have a lick of common sense."

You don't have any common sense, not right now. "About the bull dykes, I take it you think you're not one?"

"Not like them, no. I mean, you, it's obvious you're a tomboy. Those clothes you had on last night, I thought you looked way too masculine. The top you have on now, that's a little better, but you really need to let your hair grow longer on the sides."

Despite herself, Cat examined her shirt. It was a light blue cotton top with short sleeves. What made it too strong in Sherron's book? As for her hair, it wasn't a mullet, nor was it short like Tina's these days. Tina. If only Cat had the slightest clue how to carry on a non-book conversation with her. Instead, she was stuck on her own territory with this clueless femme.

"The only difference between you and a butch is surface, that's all." Not that she was an expert on the subject, Cat realized, but she knew more than her guest. "In fact, I don't know if you're aware of this, but there's a whole world of lesbians out there. I've heard there's even a gay church in Lubbock. I bet they'd love for you to sing there, and I've got news for you, you're seriously gay. I haven't been with anyone since I was seventeen, but you've been running after women for years. How many have there been? Can you tell me that?"

Sherron couldn't meet her eyes. "That I've been interested in?"

"Sure, that. Or ones you've gone to bed with."

Sherron's fingers idly traced out an unplayed chord.

Cat cast her eyes toward the near wall, where Neil had plastered a couple of promotional photographs, one of Cat by herself and another of her with the band.

Things were moving along for her, career-wise. The current conversation, however, remained stalled at a Dallas-traffic-jam pace.

"Three. Maybe the last one I shouldn't count because we didn't do anything, but we kissed." More to herself, Sherron said softly, "Boy, did we kiss."

"And how many women have you been interested in—"

"What about you? You want to try answering questions for a change? Are you going to tell me that some girl you screwed back in high school, that's the only one you've ever been with? And I bet you chased the dog out of her. I bet she didn't have a chance, did she?"

Cat had no reply at first, for she did pursue Dani. She kissed her behind some spindly trees at Palo Duro Canyon one evening where their church teen group had gone to celebrate their carwash fundraiser.

Dani didn't fight it. She wasted little time inviting Cat over to her father's house, where she was living at the time due to her parents' messy divorce proceedings, and the following weekend their fumblings turned more intense.

Dani asked me out, she thought, but I as much as promised her the moon if she did, and back then, I played up my femme side, although not with near the polish of Sherron, present moment excepted.

"Only one. So far. And yes, I've looked since then. I just never pursued. It'd be stupid to try anything in this town. You know that."

Cat quit Marta's bowling team because Marquetta Benson, who also worked at the hospital—too small a town, much too small a town—got into Cat's head. Marquetta had a few extra pounds, but well placed. She was so lushly vivid, like the human embodiment of a ripe summer peach, that Cat couldn't take her eyes off of her. And then there was Tina...

"Yes, I've been tempted."

"Woo-hoo. Tempted. The saint speaks. In the meantime, I can't stay in that house forever. It's in Ryan's name, and you can best believe while he may be fair about what's in it, the house is staying with him. After all, he has a daughter to raise."

Sherron tried, but failed, to contain her tears. Cat scrounged up some tissues for her.

"What kills me is that Emily's going to think I'm okay with this." Sherron's face was flushed under the tan. "Ryan said it's best she think he and I don't love each other anymore and that I want her to be with him since I'll be going back to school. He said he'd pay for it, if you can believe that."

"You don't want your daughter to know you're gay?"

"She's going to hate me enough. I'm not going to add that on. Ryan doesn't want her to find out. He's afraid it might warp her somehow. I'd rather not tell my parents, but I don't see how I can avoid it."

Cat thought about their lawyer in Lubbock, who was a man Neil dated many years ago. He was discreet and ran a successful practice. She knew he had other clients in Tantona, but with any kind of luck, not Ryan.

"It sounds to me like you need a lawyer who'll keep the details quiet but not let you get totally shafted in the divorce decree. I know someone who can help."

Cat looked at the gratitude in Sherron's eyes. *No one has to find out how Sherron hired her fancy lawyer.*

Yesterday, they barely knew each other, and now she was looking at Cat as though they were new best friends. This would not go over well with Neil, she suspected, but what else could she do? She had talked to Ryan, and even if it wasn't her fault, per se, she did give the man a bit of a shove.

Mouth shut, Cat, from now on.

Chapter 11

Mandy was working her third straight evening shift, and again her instructions were to float in Chris Delgado's wake, draw blood, and pay attention when he ran tests in the lab. Given Mandy's limited experience, it all seemed routine, until the ambulance arrived with Ricky Garcia, who had overdosed.

Mandy drew the blood from her fellow prayer circle member then darted out of range before he puked over everyone in attendance. LaSonda Kindred, a granite slice displeased about having to cover for a sick colleague, barked out orders that, to Mandy, were still half-gibberish, half-English, but becoming more understandable in the weeks since she'd started working at the hospital.

She noticed Otilia Garcia and her husband standing by the entrance, obviously upset about their son. She wanted to go over and reassure them, but Marta Horton had already bawled her out for doing something like that her first day on the job.

Back in the lab, Mandy took a moment to call Tina about Ricky. By the time she came back to ER, she saw Tina sitting in the waiting room across the hall with the Garcias.

As for the source of her current employment, Mandy heard through the grapevine that Sherron was going through a painful divorce—was there any other kind?—and living in a house not far from Tina's duplex.

She figured that the three of them wouldn't be hanging out much together, although Tina proclaimed herself free of jealousy on that count. Mandy thought if anyone should be jealous, it should be herself. Tina got to go to bed with Sherron, a fact Mandy tried not to think about, particularly the part about Sherron.

Something else worried her, to the point that she kept secretly checking Tina for danger signs, even asking the neuro resident on call last night for insight into Huntington's Disease. He rattled off the symptoms, which ranged from dreadful to atrocious, then asked why she was interested. Mandy had made a noncommittal response.

Ricky didn't seem any more alert when she gave the doctor the results, but upon seeing Mandy, he shot her a look of pure hatred. She broke several hospital policies in as many steps.

"Do you want me to contact Brother Jesse?"

"Why? You haven't been going. He'd just tell me to pray." His voice came out blurry.

"That's not a bad idea."

"You don't believe in it. He said you were sick, that you're going to hell."

"He's wrong. I'm healthy for the first time in my life. I know that God loves me, and he loves me just as I am."

Ricky turned his head away.

In the next room, Mandy drew blood from Sadie Inkston, a frail nursing home resident who seemed clear-headed, considering she had been scooped off her bathroom floor after a fall. The hip X-ray showed a suspicious mass. Sadie diagnosed it immediately.

"Cancer doesn't run through my family. It gallops."

* * *

Rico Garcia, a burly man with a weathered face, aimed his words at the emergency room entrance across the hall. "That damned preacher said Ricky was doing better. He lied, he lied through his teeth. He said we didn't need to take him to doctors, said they couldn't do anything for him, but where are we? Where are we? In a hospital."

Ricky could have tried harder, Tina supposed. He had swallowed his mother's muscle relaxants and a full bottle of prescription cough syrup, but it was enough to land him in a hospital bed. If Tina had known Ricky was that fragile, she could have been helpful before this night, but Otilia didn't share personal details. Mandy never spent any one-on-one time with the boy in prayer circle. Even now, Otilia brushed aside Tina's attempts at compassion.

"We'll check him out in the morning and take him to San Antonio. He can stay with my sister. He'll meet a good girl there instead of the sluts up here." Otilia spoke with her usual snap, but the strain in her eyes showed.

Tina tried again. "He's not sick, and you can't blame the girls here. You can't. He's gay, that's all."

"No," Rico shouted, drawing attention from LaSonda across the hall, who frowned at them.

"You can blame it on the local girls, or you can love your son, love him the way he is." Tina spoke with more acid in her voice than she had intended. "If you do that, you might still be talking to him in five years—that is, if he's still alive."

"I'll see you at work Monday." Otilia refused to back down, but Rico appeared devastated.

There was nothing more Tina could do, so she drove home. Strolling up the sidewalk, she saw Becca through her open door, talking to Sherron.

Tina could hear "Shelly's Winter Love," a Merle Haggard song covered by the Maines Brothers, playing on Becca's stereo. The lyrics described a mysteriously troubled woman, and the song was one of her favorites, a fact Sherron well knew, since that was the song playing when Sherron first took her to bed.

"Oh, there you are." Becca waved her inside. "I wondered where you were at."

Gracie Munoz, in a longer pair of shorts and an actual blouse this time, sat at the kitchen table. From her smile, she seemed to have forgiven Tina for her obtuseness.

"I feel like dancing," Sherron said.

"There's no room," Becca said, but she went into Sherron's arms without protest. They assayed a mini-waltz in the living room.

Sherron looked over her shoulder at Tina. "I brought most of a twelve-pack and chips 'n dip. Becca said your girlfriend would be off at eleven. I decided to bring over a party."

In a matter of weeks, Sherron had turned into a country-dancing beer drinker, albeit with impeccable styling and pressed jeans.

How did Sherron know Becca was gay? Tina suspected that Sherron just winged it instead of relying on a series of ever-more-suggestive comments. Splitting up with her husband at least changed her approach to meeting women.

* * *

The Tantona Tigers lost by only one touchdown to Lubbock Cooper, so Neil and Cat agreed the night had been a success.

Wesley claimed higher standards. "I'm going out for the team next year. They could do worse than me."

Neil and Cat eyed each other. Wesley, already over six foot tall, was being actively recruited for junior varsity basketball, despite having learned some of his moves from Cat, who, lesbian stereotype aside, possessed limited skills. Her father refused to let her play organized sports in high school, claiming proper girls didn't perspire. Neil, a Brookeland basketball standout, knew what he was doing, but played too rough.

Football struck her as a good way to wreck a knee, which made her sound disinterested, at best.

"We'll see come next spring, but if you want to play basketball, we're okay with that." The phone was ringing as they entered the kitchen.

Neil listened to the receiver for a moment and then handed it over to Cat. Wesley pretended to throw a pass in their direction and headed down the hallway.

"Where have you been?" She heard Sherron shout through the sound of a Rosanne Cash song.

"We just got back from the football game."

"You should be here."

"It's kind of late."

"I'm over at Becca Reyes's apartment. Tina's here and Mandy will be in later. Come on over. It won't kill you." Sherron hung up.

This was the same hollow-eyed woman Cat had seen days ago in United Supermarket produce section, mechanically picking out tomatoes. Cat thought about saying hello, but Sherron seemed so withdrawn. When Cat pulled her cart up to the cashier's line, she understood why. Two women ahead of her, one of whom she recognized from her days in the Parent-Teacher Organization, were gossiping about Sherron and making no attempt to lower their voices.

"Well, I heard that Ryan wanted to have her committed to the state hospital, but Brother Jesse said that wouldn't do any good, not while the devil's in control of her," PTO Mother said. A bubble-haired redhead, she had a cart full of frozen dinners and a mind loaded with preservatives.

"People like her need to be locked up," her friend said. "My husband says they want to be sick. They want to wallow in the muck."

"I don't want that thing staring at me. God knows what kind of perverted ideas are in her head." PTO Mother produced an extravagant shudder.

Cat finally remembered her name. "I wouldn't worry about that, Stacie. I doubt you're anyone's type, gay or straight."

Cat abandoned her cart and heard the women gasp behind her as she headed for the door. She came home that night with take-out pizza. Given the stormy expression on her face, Neil knew better than to ask her what was the matter.

Sherron must have decided that if she had to wallow, she'd do it with her fellow muckees. Ryan had so far kept his mouth shut about Cat's admission, or at least nothing had reached her through the grapevine, but Sherron surely had told the women. Otherwise, why else would Cat be invited to the party?

"It's a little get-together at Becca's," she said to Neil. "Tina's there, and Sherron. Mandy's on her way."

She could not feel more intimidated if Martina Navratilova and the Pope were in the living room playing two-handed Spades.

"Go." Neil gave her a supportive smile. "It's just a little get-together. Go have some fun. You've been working so hard lately, and tomorrow's the Eckerts' party. No rest for the weary. You might as well go see the gals."

"I don't know what to say to them." *Or do, or think*. She hadn't a clue.

"Go. I'll be so disappointed if you don't at least try."

Chapter 12

Mandy sat on Becca's sofa next to Tina, failing in her effort to look on the bright side.

Realistically speaking, since Sherron was bound to pay her a visit at some point, at least she did appear to have her sights set on the hostess this evening. Sherron made a point of it, in fact, like she knew there were people in the room who had reason to be wary of her motives. Daddy always said there was a wild card in any deck.

The wild card wasn't near as rambunctious as she pretended. Since Mandy walked in, Sherron had yet to take a sip from the beer can she kept hauling around. First, she teased a *cumbia* dance lesson out of Gracie, then she prevailed upon Mandy to describe the highlights of her evening's work. She listened intently to the Garcia case from a chair pulled close to Becca and as far from Mandy as the room allowed.

"There are soft drinks in the fridge if anyone wants them." Becca smiled when Sherron leaped at the offer.

"As much as I respect Otilia's work ethic, she wouldn't be my choice for the most enlightened parent in Tantona." Tina appeared not to notice the Sherron byplay.

"No, really?" Becca said with mock surprise. She was interrupted by a knock on the door.

Becca welcomed Cat Acuff and placed her in a chair next to Tina. Cat said little but had no problem knocking down a beer.

Mandy couldn't understand why the lady was so tense. Other than possibly Gracie, she was acquainted with everyone. Cat was wearing a black camisole and a pair of blue jeans that failed to disguise a killer set of legs. How good it felt to honestly admire another woman without Brother Jesse's alarm bell going off.

Cat tapped one foot nervously during Gracie's recap of a party she and Becca attended many years ago at Barbara and Darlene's house. For Gracie, that had been the only other gay party she ever attended in Tantona.

Party, however, sounded like an overstatement. Besides the four mentioned, the only other people in attendance were the former drama teacher, his cop-boyfriend from Lubbock, and a married ex-lover of Barbara's, who showed up long enough to get run off by Darlene. Gracie started to say the ex-lover's name, but Becca shook her head.

"Barbara Wolfe?" Cat's voice was a notch closer to audible. "My band's playing LaSonda's party tomorrow night, and Mary said Barbara and Darlene would be there."

"Oh, good," Becca said. "I guess LaSonda and Barbara are working things out."

Mandy wanted to ask how it was Becca got to be on speaking terms with them, since she had never managed more than a stiff hello to Darlene at the grocery store, forget about the far more intimidating Barbara, but the conversation took another turn.

Cat invited Tina, then everyone else, to the show. "I'm sure Mary won't mind 'cause she knows all of you anyway. I'll call her tomorrow."

"Thanks, but Mary sent me an invitation," Becca said. "Gracie said she'd come along to keep me company."

"Mary called me a few days ago," Sherron said. "She wanted to make sure I knew Ryan wouldn't be there."

Ryan's an asshole, Mandy thought. Sherron made a lot of mistakes but still…

"And Mandy's coming with me, so we're all covered," Tina said. "Thanks for thinking of me. I appreciate it."

* * *

Tina and Cat smiled at each other, their eyes lingering on one another, then the smiles grew wider. Maybe it was because they were sitting in a lesbian's apartment with fellow lesbians, and it felt so frigging normal.

Also normal was Mandy's fidgety attention span. One moment she inspected Tina's Coors consumption—minimal—then the next moment, she checked Tina for signs of Huntington's decrepitude. The rest of the time, she gawked at Sherron, as though Tina couldn't tell what was going on between them. It was like high school all over again.

Well, she could say that, but her high school years were spent in class, working at Rosen's Department Store, or helping take care of her brother. Tina worked all the way through college, and even after coming to teach at Tantona High School, she still put in hours after school filling in for Dad at the store.

When Rosen's closed, Mom died, and Dad moved to Houston, she felt free to pursue her own dreams in life. But what dreams did she have by then? None that she could think of. Then the librarian position came open. She thought the library board hired her because she fit the stereotype: responsible, fashion-challenged, and intelligent.

So now she sat, both a feckless teen and the world's oldest crone, nominally dating someone who couldn't keep her eyes off Sherron Steinhall, that wellborn spitfire.

Sherron, Becca, and Gracie clustered in the kitchen, laughing at Gracie's attempts to create a margarita mix from scratch. Ice, a blender, tequila, one lime, and much fortitude were her key ingredients.

Tina watched Mandy watch Sherron, then came to a decision.

"Go talk to her," she said to Mandy. She tried to avoid sounding irritated. They had been together by virtue of proximity and friendship, not due to any strong attraction.

"Huh?" Mandy had a guilty look on her face. "I'm okay here."

"I don't have dibs on you, and it's obvious the two of you still have feelings for each other. Go talk to her."

Mandy sat there, seeming paralyzed by indecision. Stronger measures were needed. By Tina's count, Cat was working on her third beer and studiously paying attention to the kitchen crew.

"Cat, come with me, I have a book I want to show you." Tina led Cat from the room. Next door, Tina listened to Cat go on at length about Kawabata's *Snow Country*, how she wanted to read it but hadn't gotten around to ordering via interlibrary loan. With one last swallow, Cat crumpled the can then looked abashed.

"Wow, I don't usually drink that fast."

"A little while back, I had a lost weekend all in one night." Tina took the can from her guest and walked it to the kitchen trashcan. "That's how Mandy and I ended up dating."

Tina always applied a strict level of professionalism around Mrs. Acuff, never allowing an ethical hair out of place. So now, when it was safe to have an actual emotion about Cat, why was she talking about blackouts and drunken misbehavior?

It's not as though I have a chance with someone like her, Tina thought. But those eyes, almond-shaped, and obsidian black. Even when Cat's a bit loaded, swathed in subdued lighting, there's something in her eyes that draws a person in, draws them closer.

Cat worked on a cup of coffee and her anxiety level at the same time. This was the closest she had ever been to Tina without a crowd of dancers or a thousand books nearby. It didn't seem as though Tina and Mandy had gotten serious about each other, to judge by Tina's elliptical statements. Maybe that was due to the difference in their ages and personalities, or maybe due to something else.

"You said she worried about you. Because of your getting drunk that night?"

To Cat's way of thinking, Tina possessed a delicate nose and a mouth always ready to smile, even willing to laugh at herself over her recent behavior. The smile disappeared from Tina's face.

"I told her something personal about me. She has a caring side, and I suppose that's what I responded to. But the flip side of that is, it's what she sees about me now: the potential problem. If we'd tried to know each other gradually over a few dates, and then she found out, maybe it would've been different. We got off on the wrong foot."

"Oh, I wouldn't put it all on the Huntington's. She connects with Sherron. They're a couple of backsliding church girls. They have more in common than one might think."

Tina stared at her. "How do you…?"

Neil's great-aunt took a long time fading at the nursing home, long enough that Cat had several opportunities to see Tina in the last year with her mother.

She overheard nurse's aides talking about Tina, saying that her brother died of the same disease. Tina was a good daughter; that is, someone willing to clean bedpans and dodge blows. Later, the staff speculated about why Tina's father ended up taking his wife home right before she died. Cat didn't see the need in bringing up that subject.

Once Cat explained the nursing home connection to her, Tina still looked puzzled.

"I guess I shouldn't be surprised that you would have heard about the problem. It's not as though it's a state secret. I don't remember you ever being at the nursing home, though."

"All those patients' family members going in and out, why would you?"

"Because." Tina's face flushed. "Because I can't take my eyes off of you, that's why."

"I'm no Sherron," Cat said with a laugh.

"She's overrated, believe me. When I was in college, I slept around some but went right back in the closet. Sherron brought me out a couple of years ago, so I guess I should thank her."

Tina changed the music to soft jazz, then she collected their cups for refills. When she sat back down, Cat moved in a few degrees.

It should have been me. Cat thought. All those years of lurking in the stacks to catch a glimpse of you unaware, and all that time I wondered about you, I longed for you. Sherron had the nerve to try first, but it should have been me.

"And about the night of the show, when we danced?" she asked. Time to put it all out there. "I mean, first time in a gay bar since I was seventeen, and it felt like Neil was trying to run things, and I'm sorry. I bailed."

She was so close, feeling the warmth of Tina's arm stretched along the top of the sofa. So close.

"I couldn't tell whether you wanted to dance or not." Tina spoke in her bland, librarian voice.

"Are you kidding? I wanted to from the get-go, but Neil was being too much of a booster. He's been pushing me lately to meet people. Tonight, he helped in a good way. Believe me, I have no problem being here with you."

Tina placed her cup on the table and said, "If you don't kiss me, I will explode, right here, right now."

If Cat moved right now, she would fall apart. It had been so long ago since those Amarillo nights with Dani, bringing forth images of a teenager she couldn't even recognize anymore.

Cat slowly leaned forward to kiss Tina's lips, which even then were smiling back at her.

Did Tina notice Cat's entire body was shaking like a willow tree during a blue norther, and about as sturdy? If Tina did, she said nothing as she softly traced the arc of Cat's arm as it folded over her breast.

A few years later, the phone rang. It was Neil, saying that there was no need to come on home just yet. He planned to tell Wesley when he got up in the morning that Mom was out running errands. The moment slipped away.

Tina busied herself in the kitchen while Cat struggled to address her husband in a civil manner. Off the phone, Cat stalked over to Tina and drew her away from the sink.

"I know, I know tonight's not quite working for us, but be ready, would you, for after the show tomorrow? We're doing one set as a full band, then Mimi and I are going to debut some songs we've been working on. You and me, we're not through talking, or anything else."

Tina nodded once, her eyes brimming, and then relaxed into Cat's arms.

Chapter 13

While Sherron didn't live in a duplex, the house was small enough to qualify as one, what with two small bedrooms and a cramped kitchen. Even so, the attached garage and a roofed back porch took it a step up from Mandy's place. The one good outcome to Sherron's decline in property value was that Mandy could see her in more relaxing surroundings.

Sherron's furniture, most of it from her well-to-do parents and brothers, tended toward tans and browns, except for a blazing forest green recliner, upon which Mandy was waiting. Mandy wished her date would get a move on so they could make it to the party on time.

Sherron called from the bedroom, "Don't worry. Cat said it would start at eight, but the band kicks off at nine. There's plenty of time. You just don't want to miss the cake."

"And you don't want to be around LaSonda, you homewrecker."

"Oh, that," Sherron said airily. "LaSonda saw me in the snack bar the other day and said she heard I'm a lesbian. She understands I was trying to cover my tracks at the barbecue, but now that everybody knows, she doesn't think it's necessary for me to go after her husband. That sounded reasonable, I thought."

So much for Sherron having one toe in the closet. Ryan's sister, in reaction to Sherron hiring a lawyer, or perhaps her own evil spite, spread the story far and wide, including the part where Sherron came on to Neil Acuff.

Last night, Mandy sat up with Sherron at her house eating popcorn and hearing what had been going on with the divorce. The initial filing called for Ryan to retain sole custody. Until she had her day in court, Sherron was enjoined from being in Emily's presence.

Sherron told her that she plotted routes that might take her "accidentally" near Emily—her friends' houses, Pizza Hut, McDonald's, the church—but she had already been stopped half a block from Ryan's house on suspicion of violating the court order. The officer told her charges would be filed the next time.

According to Sherron, she had one friend left in the business office, Marquetta Benson, whose daughter went to school with Emily. According to Marquetta, Emily appeared to be doing about as well as could be expected.

From Mandy's point of view, the whole mess could have been avoided if she hadn't sent Sherron home in tears that night.

Sometimes people are better off with their illusions. As long as Sherron could pretend to herself that she was more or less straight, she could pretend with Ryan, which meant no confession, no divorce proceedings, and no stolen daughter.

Just when Mandy was about to make another plea for speed, Sherron came out of the bedroom in a black, lattice-pattern, strapless dress with a gold chain belt and heels.

"Hey, good lookin'." Sherron wore a satisfied smile. "You have on the clothes I picked out."

"Didn't you say you'd go alone if I didn't?"

"I might have said that."

Mandy's outfit consisted of black gabardine slacks, a black tank a size too small that Sherron said flattered her twin assets, and a gold raw silk blouse, worn open, with a red Chinese dragon on the back. The slacks had been purchased that afternoon in Lubbock and the blouse rescued from the back of Sherron's closet, unworn, since Ryan hated it.

It hit Mandy that they were dressed as a couple and would be seen as such at a party in Tantona, no less, so by tomorrow, Ryan would know, then his lawyer, then the judge.

"You've given up, haven't you, on getting your daughter back," Mandy said.

"Heck, no. My lawyer called before you came over. Ryan's shyster said that if I tried for joint custody, he'd drag Tina into it and make her an issue. Shows I have a history. You, I figure you can handle the heat. Marta doesn't care who you sleep with, but if that crabby old judge hears about Tina, I'll be lucky if I ever see Emily again."

Tina, then, would be looking for a new job, and not likely to find it in Tantona.

"What are you going to do?" Mandy asked.

There was a slight wobble in Sherron's voice, then came the steel.

"I told him to make the deal. I'm allowed supervised visits for the next six months, then I'll get one weekend a month and alternate holidays. A year of that, then I'll have her every other weekend and two weeks in the summer. Ryan gets the house and half the furnishings—let me finish."

Sherron picked up her purse and strode out the door, carrying Mandy in her wake.

"Ryan agreed not to make any conditions about my personal life. Whoever I'm seeing, and as far as I'm concerned it dang well better be you, he can't say squat about it. The only thing is that when Emily's in the house, no female can be in my bed."

Mandy hastened to get into the passenger seat of Sherron's Town Car, feeling as though she had been force-marched through a wind tunnel. Once on the road, she at last entered the conversation.

"He agreed to that? You gave up everything for that?"

Giving her head a slight, rueful shake, Sherron kept her eyes forward.

"I never thought I could get Emily back for good. I did hope for joint custody, but Ryan's not going to let that happen. I know that now. I just didn't think he had any right to tell me who I could see. Ryan knew before we got married I'd been with a woman, and he knew who she was."

"Who?"

"I'll never tell anyone unless he goes back on his word."

Three cars pulled out of the south drive as they pulled into the north drive. Mandy wondered aloud, "Are we late?"

"No. They had the official birthday party and barbecue early so the kids could come. I imagine some people aren't staying for the grown-up hootenanny. Don't worry, I'm sure there's plenty of cake left."

"What is up with you and that cake?"

Mandy tapped her on the shoulder playfully as Sherron found a spot next to a long, black, Dodge pickup that looked familiar. Sherron turned to Mandy and deposited a kiss on her lips.

"I don't think you've had enough cake in your life. I'm here to make sure you never miss out again."

Another kiss like that, and they would be no-shows.

As they walked around the last corner to the Eckerts' alfalfa-green back lawn, Mandy stopped for a moment to sniff the air.

"That's Erlinda's barbecue, or I'll eat my hat. In fact, Erlinda could barbecue my hat, and I'd eat every bite."

On the south side of the lawn beside the Eckerts' triple-car garage, a scowling Erlinda and a polar-opposite Hilario were chopping up brisket and sausage to recycle them into wraps. There were ample remains of a fluorescent blue and yellow cake on a separate table.

The source of Hilario's good humor, Tommy Williams, occupied a folding chair on spectators' row, where partygoers watched the band setting up in front of the garage. Tommy sat next to Sydney Melston, who had a glass of white wine in her hand, the bottle next to her feet. Were Tommy and Sydney play-pretend back together, Mandy wondered mildly.

She was more interested in the presence of Barbara Wolfe and Darlene, standing next to LaSonda and her husband by a barrel of iced bottles of beer. The mood seemed pleasant, yet Mandy still didn't think she could muster the courage to speak to Barbara.

Mandy recalled the time Senator Phil Gramm came to Tantona, his aides rustling the media through a half-hour press opportunity. Photograph this, write that, hurry up, hurry up, and get the hell out. Barbara is the senior member, so respect is not only due, but overdue.

Except that Gramm stood there with the seized drug raid prop, a shotgun, faking a forceful presence that Barbara possessed naturally, so maybe not the best comparison.

Maybe she was more like a Martin Luther King, who got arrested for DWI back in the day, or maybe a butch Loretta Lynn, in her current getup of western suit slacks, a short-sleeved white shirt and patchwork vest.

Mandy always thought of Barbara as a looming presence, but she seemed smallish next to LaSonda. Her daughter could make a lot of women seem spindly, not to mention LaSonda's slip of a husband. Darlene, attired in an attractive blue frock, stood by Barbara with a tranquil expression on her face.

"There's Becca," Sherron said merrily, and off they went to say hello, not bothering with formal greetings to the hosts, Barlow and Mary Eckert. Sherron plowed her own acre in life.

Becca was standing by a pink crepe myrtle and chatting with Gracie and Tina. It occurred to Mandy that there were several gay people at the party. Now that she actually knew who they were, it came as something of a surprise.

At some point, Mandy needed to say something to Tina, but she had no idea how to phrase the apology. I'm sorry it's so obvious I have a thing for Sherron. I'm sorry I ran away from you and your problem the first chance I got. Tina didn't know about the last part and didn't need to ever find out.

To be honest, she didn't think all of Tina's behavior when she got plastered that night was because of the booze, and while she could be wrong, she thought maybe Tina was starting to show... signs.

It could be Mandy's imagination, the worry talking, but Tina did try to open her car door that night while they were hurtling down the road a mile a minute. It might have been the alcohol or that disease. And didn't she act goofy-strange the other night? All Mandy knew was she didn't have a boatload of money and endless free hours to take care of Tina if the problem did come up. Mandy couldn't risk getting involved, which made her, whether she liked it or not, just like Daddy and about as worthless.

"Baby, cheer up. It's a party, don't you know?" Sherron gave her a hug in front of God and everybody.

* * *

To Tina, they were like a beautiful, contrasting pair of ponies, stunning in gold and black, right down to their hair colors. Sherron's mode of coming out tonight, even though pushed out of the closet, even when she had to be terrified of losing her child, was to be flagrantly, defiantly bold.

Tina had thought of her as being deceitful with her husband, and Tina's guilt over the affair was in part the reason why she broke up with Sherron. Both the affair and the marriage had been a mistake, but Sherron had Mandy now. Seeing the pair together, Tina couldn't visualize herself with either of them. With Cat, however, Tina's imagination worked at a feverish pace.

Earlier, Tina broke her self-made promise to keep away from Cat before the show, but Cat welcomed her visit in the garage, where they hid behind a boat.

Tina broke them apart. "I'm nothing but a distraction right now. You need to get ready."

Cat gave her a reckless smile. "You're getting me ready just standing there."

Instead of the usual jagged-edged rock goddess, Cat was turned out in a pair of lavender slacks and a soft white shirt with the sleeves rolled up. Her waves of black hair had been given a relaxed style that Neil still probably slaved over.

Now, Tina was standing a short distance away from Judge Walt Burlow, his wife, Roberta, and her library board president, George Bering. She wondered what George would say about what she had been up to with Cat. As much as he talked about antiques, surely he had met a few gay people. Her orientation probably wouldn't matter to him.

County Judge Walt Burlow, however, would be a different matter. His wife happened to be Ryan's aunt, with the same thoroughbred good looks and high polish, and the same concern about social appearances.

Tina was curious to see Roberta's reaction to her niece-by-marriage's escort for the night, so she wandered near Roberta's path, casting casual hellos toward those she passed until Roberta stopped moving.

Tina watched Roberta's head turn slowly as Sherron and Mandy passed by a few yards away, chattering nonstop with Gracie. For a few seconds Tina saw Roberta's face full on, yet her eyes were filled not with disgust, but with something like melancholy.

It had to mean that the Steinhalls were not united in their loathing of Sherron. Tina planned to share that piece of intelligence with Sherron, as she could use an ally in that family.

As Cat marched up to the microphone, Tina saw Syd lurch from her chair and walk toward the patio, likely en route to the bathroom.

With an abrupt change in direction, she reached Tina at roughly the same time as Neil and Becca did. Tina thought about leaving, but in her peripheral vision, she saw Mary Eckert talking to the Rosens. It would be so very nice not to create a scene.

Syd leaned down into Tina's face—the band's cover of the Replacements' "I'll Be You" made an odd counterpoint—and said in a surly tone, "Tommy and I are getting married next month. It's at the country club. You're not invited."

"Syd." Becca placed her hand on Syd's arm. "Come with me. I want to talk to you about something going on at school."

"What kind of talking, Becca?" Syd flung Becca's hand away. "Like what you've been doing with Tina? Most people would call it screwing. Is that what you're wanting to do, Becca? Why didn't you—you've never, ever wanted to talk to me before, and we were working together everyday."

Tina and Becca shot flustered looks at one another. Syd must have timed her drive-bys to miss Mandy. More likely, she preferred to see Becca as her rival or temptation. Rage clotted Syd's voice as she refocused on Tina. "All you had to do was answer the phone."

"You're right. I should have told you it was over instead of letting it slide. But I tried talking to you before. You kept brushing me off. You didn't think there was a problem. I did. You wanted to totally hide in the closet. I didn't. I'm sorry that my manners suck. I should have called, but you didn't care about me anyway, so what did it matter?"

Tina didn't want to explain, didn't want to deal with Syd another second longer. Being kind was no kindness at all. Syd had stopped the phone calls, but evidently she needed to quit driving by the apartment.

Tommy joined them, flanking Syd from the left, Neil from the right.

"That's right. I didn't give a damn about you." Syd tried to bring her arms up only to find them pinned by Tommy and Neil.

"I'm not— Shit, Neil, I'm not going to hit her, though the slut deserves it."

"You watch your mouth," Becca said.

Neil took charge. "Ladies, let's all watch our mouths. I recommend using the mirror in the bathroom to do just that. Closest one, as I recall, is through the patio."

Neil's voice seemed perfectly pitched to cut through the noise and yet not be overheard by the rest of the party. It might have been a trick he picked from speaking to customers with heads under hairdryers.

"I'll move when I'm damn well ready."

Neil pressed into Syd, his hand tight on her arm. He had a hard, unfamiliar expression on his face.

"I'm ready to give you the worst haircut of your life, so you better come with us and make it look like we're the best of friends, because if you don't, you'll regret it. I won't let you ruin this night."

That shut her up enough so that Tommy and Neil, smiles plastered on their faces, could take Syd inside.

Told to stay behind, the friends shook their heads at each other as Gracie and then Mary Eckert arrived. Becca was the first to break into a nervous laugh, joined by Tina and then good-natured Gracie, who didn't care what the joke was about.

"What's up with Syd? I've never seen her that upset before," Gracie said in a near bellow, then the song stopped.

"You know how it is with ex-girlfriends, Gracie," Mary drawled. "They don't always take rejection in a ladylike manner."

"Don't I know it," Gracie said easily, as though she had been out to Mary for ages. "Barbara went crazy on me for a while, but then Darlene made her feel all better."

It took Tina a moment to figure out what she was hearing. Gracie and Barbara Wolfe used to be an item, and not only that, Mary appeared to have the lowdown on several couples.

"All I know, Becca, is that it was about time you two quit being just neighbors. I thought I was going to have to bring over a connect-the-dot game so y'all would figure out you were made for each other."

Mary took a sip from her vat of coffee, appearing puzzled by the identical looks of dismay on the others' faces.

"We're not dating," Becca said, raising her voice as a new number started. "Tina's interested in someone else right now."

And Gracie, Tina noticed, wanted Becca, which put her in the same category as Syd. This surely would help Becca get over her ex-lover.

Mary seemed disappointed, then her face brightened as she turned to Tina. "Who are you going out with?"

"It's in the early stages. I don't want to jinx it," Tina explained haltingly. Barlow Eckert and the Rosens arrived, allowing Becca and Gracie to step away.

Ostensibly, it was to get closer to the band—dancing had broken out near the garage—but Tina could see Gracie move closer to Becca the farther away they went.

Although Tina saw Estelle Rosen now and then at the library, she hadn't seen Arthur in years. Decades older than Estelle, he looked to be in his eighties, white-haired, yet with erect posture and alert, glittering eyes. He had always seemed old to Tina, even back when she visited the store as a child, long before she became Dad's stand-in.

"Tell me about the barbecue," Arthur said. "Would you eat it in a restaurant and buy it in a store?"

"Definitely. I've had Erlinda's sauce before." Mandy kept a supply in her refrigerator.

"I don't know why that family of hers hasn't given her a storefront," Estelle complained.

"She's a woman, that's why. *El Jefe* Aldaiz won't put a dime into something his favored sons aren't a part of. That's why we're stepping in," Mary said.

The "we" consisted of the Eckerts, the Rosens, and several other investors. Extensive remodeling of the Rosens' shuttered store lay ahead, with the restaurant slated to open next spring, but Taste Tantona Inc. had bigger plans. Bottling and packaging equipment was already on order for installation in a warehouse Tommy owned, which would house their production line of barbecue sauces.

Tina saw the real benefit to Tommy. Hilario could run a restaurant and come close to equaling his sister in the kitchen. Tommy lucked into an acceptable way to be near his lover in public.

Estelle Rosen said, with her typical enthusiasm, "Barlow and Arthur are looking at some properties in Lubbock for when we're ready to franchise. All we need is a full-time CEO."

"You could do that easily enough," Tina said.

"Sweetie, we're moving end of the year to San Diego to be near the grandkids. No, we need someone who'll have the time and energy to keep after it all the time. During the winter, Tommy can be more active, but right now he's busy with the harvest, and Mary has enough going on as it is."

As she spoke, Estelle gave Tina a measured appraisal that had nothing to do with the topic at hand. Everyone who knew Tina's family, who knew the history at all, at some point gave her the look, but Estelle tried to be subtle about it.

Tina thought about Cat for the position. She was busy right now, and if Tina had anything to say about it, about to become even busier. Tina knew exactly the right person for the job.

"You need someone who'll present well, who knows her numbers, and is connected in Lubbock, because I agree with you, the real money for you, restaurant-wise, is going to be in Lubbock, and your first big market will be there."

"Sherron Steinhall." Barlow Eckert's face beamed.

Mary and Tina both stared at him.

Mary let out a guffaw. "Sugar, for once you took the words out of my mouth. Sherron knows money, let me tell you. Her daddy's a big mover-and-shaker in Lubbock, and as for folks here, they'll come to the restaurant just hopin' they'll see Sherron do something spicy, and then they'll come back for the food."

As one, the group turned their heads and watched Sherron on the bandstand sharing a vocal with Cat on "Do You Wanna Dance."

Blue Movie was playing something most of the people at the party could tap their feet to. Tina needed to get back to being Cat's groupie for the night.

The band set had come off well with few mistakes, but now the act was reduced to Cat and Mimi with the debut of their jazz set. Tina sat on the front row, looking undamaged from the set-to with Sydney.

Neil rubbed the back of Cat's neck. "You'll do fine. These people danced their butts off to your alien rock. You know they'll love hearing something familiar."

"That's just it. They've heard these songs, so they'll know if I'm doing them wrong," Cat said.

Where was Mimi? She had disappeared after the last note of the first set.

"You'll do them your way. Oh, and Tommy carted La Syd off to the pickup a little bit ago."

"She's lucky I saw you headed over to help Tina." Her neck tensed up again, despite Neil's ministrations. "If I ever see that woman again, she better hope to have Tommy with her. She'll need the protection."

"Ooh, little miss butch rears her handsome head."

"Don't start."

"It's been something, this party. It looks to me like Mary invited everyone she thinks is family here."

Before Cat could respond, she saw Mimi and Marco come out from behind the boat all aglow and a bit disheveled.

Since Cat knew Mimi didn't smoke pot—recalling her numerous turndowns of Vonn—that could only mean her keyboard player had been heterosexual all along. Maybe the two wanted to keep their relationship quiet, since didn't Marco have a soon-to-be-ex-wife over in New Mexico? Whatever the reason, it didn't matter, not anymore.

"Oh," she said with a start. "I need to go call Marta and see how Wesley's doing."

"I did that while I was in the house a little bit ago. Felix sent the girls off to a church skating party, and when they get back, there's no way Kendra will be able to sneak into Wesley's room tonight. Felix is sleeping in the den, so Kendra would have to get past Daddy Mountain."

"Forget about that happening. It's so good of them to still let Wesley stay overnight."

"Are you kidding?" Neil stopped in mid rub. "They must thank the Lord everyday that Kale has at least one friend. I know, I know, you see them as a way for Wesley to experience a quote-unquote normal family, but they're getting something from us, too."

He had a point. Despite all the time Kale spent at the Acuffs, he still acted painfully shy.

"Anyhow, Wesley's fine. Having a good time. When he gets in tomorrow, if you're not back yet, I'll come up with something. Don't worry."

She could see Tina smiling at her and felt the tension leave her body. "All of Me" would take on an entirely new meaning tonight.

Chapter 14

"I don't know," Sherron said doubtfully. Had Sherron ever experienced second thoughts about anything?

Mandy followed after Sherron, who sailed through her front door, dumped her purse and keys on a small glass table, then headed for the bedroom.

Mandy stood by the door and continued giving her thoughts about the Taste Tantona company board's presentation after the show. Maybe presentation was too fancy a word, since it consisted of Mary running rapid-fire through her points, while everyone else sucked on their beers and nodded now and then.

"Listen, it's not like Jackie was asking you to run her barbecue joint. These people have some money behind them."

From the bedroom, Sherron said, "I'm sure Jackie would give me part ownership, which means you'd get to enjoy the perks."

"You know I don't smoke anymore."

"Better not. I'll take you higher than you've ever been. Come on in, baby."

Mandy felt strangely hesitant as she stepped into the bedroom. *So much for foreplay.*

There was Sherron, naked, and lying on her bed. Mandy had no second thought.

* * *

Tina popped the cork on a bottle of Llano Estacado Chardonnay she recently purchased on the Lubbock Strip. It had been well worth the drive, she thought as she pulled two wineglasses from her kitchen cabinet.

Cat was taking a shower, claiming that the night's performance rendered her unfit for human company, although Tina didn't smell anything but Cat's usual honeyed aroma.

But when she emerged, what would Tina say? Let's go have sex? In some ways it was easier with Syd, who controlled the agenda, and before her, Sherron, who practiced equality but had a specific itinerary and procedures to follow.

Cat came to her door as an absolute unknown, except for the fact that when she held Tina at that very counter last night, Cat acted both decisive and impulsive. Anything could happen, Tina realized, anything from not being able to perform to pulling an all-nighter.

It was enough to make her want to grab her car keys and flee. But she didn't.

Instead, she filled the glasses, then carried them to the coffee table, where she lit a candle and a stick of incense. Oh yes. She kicked off her shoes then removed her watch and earrings.

She heard the shower go off, and Cat came back into the living room, wearing the robe Tina had left for her in the bathroom.

Cat stopped in her tracks. "It's been a long time."

Her voice sounded uncertain, but her eyes contained the same haunting directness from the first time she sat on Tina's sofa.

"Come over here," Tina said softly.

Cat sat beside her and silently clasped Tina's hand.

It came to Tina that she didn't want it placid as with Syd, or scripted as with Sherron, but other than that, what? No outright roughness, but something... strong. She needed very much tonight to feel. To feel.

"Don't hold back," Tina whispered in Cat's ear. "It doesn't matter how hard or how long, but don't hold back. I can take it."

How to begin, and what did Tina mean by not holding back? Since Cat was unable to breathe at the moment, there seemed little danger of her being too hard or taking too long. She couldn't quite escape the idea that this, too, was a performance, but one in which she was expected to satisfy a very select audience.

No. She couldn't pretend to be someone else, nor could she draw on past experience from her memories as the teenager who had eager yet clumsy sex with Dani a grand total of four times. That thrill seeker had no advice to give.

She returned her glass of wine to the coaster. Finding Tina's lips, she kissed her, then began undoing buttons on her blouse.

"You have entirely too many clothes on," Cat heard herself say. How lame a remark, she thought, but with a trace of a smile, Tina loosened Cat's robe and reached inside to touch her breast. Who needs words anyhow?

Cat blew out the candle, then pulled Tina to her feet. She led them into the bedroom where the covers had been thrown back, and they finished undressing and lay down.

She kissed Tina on the shoulders with the intention of easing herself on top, only to find that Tina had other ideas. *So this is how she wants to begin.*

Sliding between Cat's thighs, Tina rose above her then slid downward, then again, and again.

"Do you like that?" Tina murmured.

In response, Cat entangled her legs around her partner, swaying with the rhythm. This felt... amazing. It wasn't what she expected, but then, what did she expect? A gentle exchange of mouths and hands, the oceanic ripples she read about in a book Neil brought home from a trip to Dallas?

They were in a position that reminded her of being with those high school boys—she barely recalled that drunken botch with Neil—yet this felt far more intense.

An ocean didn't describe it. It was more like... oh. Like she didn't need her skin anymore. Skin got in the way of all this sensation, this stirring inside she had to let out.

In a visceral rush, Cat scrambled on top, then, needing to be inside Tina, realized she was already there.

It did come down to her mouth and hands, after all, yet with it came a peeling away to another layer underneath, and then another, until there was no distance between them.

Pulling back her face, but her hand inside, Cat rocked on top of Tina, feeling exhilarated, then Tina stopped moving and began curling inward.

She was getting close, Cat thought, so she slowed the tempo only to hear Tina say in a garbled voice, "More."

More what? Okay, don't panic. Read the signs. Deeper, harder. Yes. That worked, but how much harder, how much longer?

Don't hold back, Tina had said.

Part of her dithering over technique, Cat felt Tina's body opening up inside, as though she had discovered a new passageway. Well then, could that mean—and with one last, great shudder, Tina came.

Cat gazed at Tina with dark-adapted eyes, reluctant to touch her, as though she might somehow shatter the mood. Tina limply reached out a hand, and Cat couldn't hold back any longer, burying herself in Tina's arms.

Chapter 15

It was impossible to have a Sunday pray-then-eat potluck without fried chicken, even in a gay church.

The service preceding the potluck was conducted in a small, redbrick building across from a park in Lubbock. The mix of high church communion and full-gospel singing felt jarring to Mandy.

How strange to her that the service, so conventional, so heartfelt, initially fell flat. For the first time in her life, Mandy could worship in perfect comfort. Maybe she didn't want it that cozy. When the pastor talked to the flock about the importance of commitment, not only to God but also to their partners, Mandy recognized more familiar territory.

Face it, Mandy admitted inwardly. You like for your Sunday mornings to include a dose of spiritual butt kicking.

Through with church and chicken, they drove over to Sherron's parents' house, where Mandy now had been sitting alone in Sherron's car in her parents' driveway for—she checked her watch again—well over thirty minutes. Mandy had come to the conclusion that being in a relationship involved a lot of waiting.

The Berings' two-story beige stone residence staked out a sizable section of their South Lubbock block. If Sherron's parents were as imposing as their surroundings, Mandy hoped she wouldn't be invited inside.

The lawn had nice topiary, though, and the door featured an interesting cut- and stained-glass design. Why hadn't Sherron ever said that her father was related to the high-rolling Bering family in Tantona? For that matter, why hadn't Sherron told her before the drive into Lubbock that her father, who she vaguely mentioned did something at a bank, happened to be the president? Her mother, Sherron made a point of adding, had been a teller at her father's bank before their wedding.

As for why Sherron didn't go into the family business, all she would say was that her father wanted her to have some real working experience, so after her high school graduation, he lined her up a summer job at the hospital. One thing led to another, then came marriage and the carriage, like Daddy would say.

Mandy turned off the key when the radio finished playing "Never Had It So Good" by Mary something Carpenter.

What did she really know about Sherron? True, in the early weeks of their acquaintance, the two of them spent more time praying together than sharing biographies. Last night in bed, what conversation took place was of an intensely personal nature.

This morning, there had been praying, along with a dose of inspirational singing. How was it they conquered sex and religion before learning some basic facts about each other?

Reduced in her boredom to guessing at the neighboring house's floor plan, Mandy didn't notice her visitor until there came a tap on top of the Town Car. It was Sherron's father, Doak Bering, a chisel-faced man dressed in navy dress slacks and a blue-checked shirt.

He carried in his arms a glass end table, a twin to the one in Sherron's house and the stated reason she had disappeared into the house. Mandy wrapped it in a blanket and carefully placed it in the trunk as he watched without comment.

She wasn't sure what to do next. It wasn't her table, her car, her block, or her town. What on earth was keeping Sherron?

"Nice weather we're having."

Bering nodded. He gave her a once-over with the usual chest-level freeze.

"Barlow Eckert is right: you are a looker. He called this morning to invite me in on Taste Tantona. He wanted to know what I thought about my daughter handling their operations. I already had you checked out. Your father's a drinker—"

"Not in a while."

"He's a drinker and an ex-con. Your mother is mentally retarded, and the only one of your brothers who was worth anything left years ago. You should have been gone, too, but I'm guessing you thought you made it about as far up the ladder as you were likely to get."

He didn't stop to ask if he was right. Sherron inherited more than her cheekbones from this man.

"Some daddies would have you shot on sight. Those kind of daddies would put a detective on your ass and a cop on your street until you got the hell out of this state, not just Greater Tantona."

"Sir, you got no right to talk to me like a field hand. Sherron and me—"

"My girl could have done a whole lot worse than you. But in one respect, you got lucky. Gay doesn't scare me. I've seen it before.

"Sherron, now, she has a good business opportunity in front of her. You're pretty and you carry yourself well, but it's obvious that you're a dyke. Business folk, we don't care what people do in the boudoir. You be my daughter's little sweetheart, but don't get in the way of her cutting deals. That's all I ask."

If she had any sense she would climb back into the car, let Sherron drive them home to Tantona, crawl back into her orange-carpeted closet, and never come out again. Mandy figured Doak for a father who would break her into twigs if necessary. It was hard to stare down a man who stood a foot taller, but Mandy tried.

"Mr. Bering, it's true I have a lousy family, but I don't appreciate you talking about my mother. She's none of your business. Maybe I clean up nice, but I know where I come from. I know I'm not your kind of people, even if I were a man, but if I end up hiding in the back, it'll be to make life easy on Sherron, not you. Cut your damn deals. I don't care."

Bering gave her another long appraisal, this time focusing on her face.

"I apologize for what I said about your mother. It wasn't meant to be insulting." He shook his head at her regretfully. "Fact is, I knew something like this might happen. I don't like having to bring this up, but I already worked it with Steinhall's lawyer to make the custody situation as good as it is, which isn't saying much."

"Sherron thinks she—you stepped in?"

He sighed. "My wife and I, we are not going to be cut off from our grandbaby, so even though Steinhall has Judge Souther in his pocket, I've pulled all the strings I have to give Sherron some say so. But here's the drill: you don't move in with her full time. Keep your own place. You don't want them to say y'all are cohabiting, at least not until the decree comes down and probably for a good while after that."

He pulled out a card from his pocket and handed it to Mandy.

"You have trouble paying bills, call me at work. My secretary will know to put you through."

"I don't need your money." Mandy delivered that with all the will she could muster.

"Young lady, I've already arranged to pay Sherron's lawyer, but that fool judge has to believe Emily can continue to live off the fatted calf with her mother. I know you won't intend to cost money, but shit happens. When it does, come to me first."

The front door flew open. Sherron blurred down the walk, a propane blast of indignation.

"Daddy!" she called out. "You won't believe what Mom just said."

Bering grinned at Mandy. Despite her intentions, she smiled back.

* * *

Tina woke up, painfully woke up, in the middle of making coffee. She saw coffee grounds streaming down her naked thighs. Apparently, she had been trying to straighten out a crooked filter in mid-perk, which would teach her not to do anything useful on little sleep. A few sopping paper towels proved that stronger measures were needed.

When she stepped out of the shower, she noticed red spots above her left knee, which had borne the brunt of burning caffeine. Now what she wanted, more than anything, was something to eat.

"Hey, I cleaned up in the kitchen for you and managed to work us up a couple cups of coffee." Cat was fully dressed and sitting on the side of the bed. "What happened to your leg?"

"The leg's fine, just a little hot coffee got loose. It doesn't hurt." That wasn't quite true. "I guess I'm not used to staying up late."

"Or not sleeping at all, if you're unaccustomed to visitors. I sleep with a snoring man every night, so it's easy to zonk out. I'll go fetch our coffee."

"Do you mind bringing me a bagel? They're in the bread box."

"I can do you better than that."

A little later, after Cat knocked together a breakfast of scrambled eggs and toasted bagels, they ate sitting up in bed. It felt awkward wondering when Cat would leave.

"Do you feel okay now?" Cat asked.

"A hundred percent better. So, what's on tap for you today?" She clasped Cat's free hand.

"It's my turn on fixing Sunday dinner, so I really ought to be heading out." Cat didn't move. "You should see Neil Sunday mornings, newspapers strewn from one end of the bed to the other. It's a good thing he can be a cleaning demon, because he's not the neatest person in the world."

"He okay about us?"

"Ecstatic. He thinks you're great. Well, I'm sure he put the chicken out to thaw because I told him to last night." Cat still hadn't budged an inch.

"What are the sides?"

"Huh? Oh, probably some variation on potato. Wesley hates rice, although he will deign to eat broccoli casserole if it's heavy on the cheese."

"I haven't seen your house yet." Tina gave her words a neutral, take-it-as-you-will spin.

Cat turned to her with a glorious smile on her face. "You're not too tired? I mean, big whoop, making dinner, but if you don't mind."

* * *

As she towel-dried her hair, Cat felt her husband's hands take over the job, finishing with a picking out. She couldn't help but smile at Neil, who was bursting with curiosity.

"Well?"

"Finish your newspapers," she said as they went into the bedroom.

"I can't. Your date followed you home and is cooking something that smells like gravy, which would be a first for this household."

"Correction: she didn't follow me. I drove us over here. And you and I both make gravy." She pulled on a pair of jeans and a tee.

"Caterina, if you want to call it gravy, I'll support you in your delusion, but Mom and Mama have given us lessons in remedial gravy-making for years. I'm smelling the real thing."

He wandered down the hallway, breaking his Sunday morning rule of strict bed rest. Thank goodness, he had on shorts and a tank top, as Neil tended to be a nature boy when Wesley was away.

Cat believed she could hold her own in the kitchen, but her house specialty was ironing, courtesy of Mama's rigorous training. Neil turned out excellent casseroles, but friends came to their house for drinks and conversation, not for the sparkling canapés.

Tina, on the other hand, had a knack for cooking, at least for fried chicken, mashed potatoes and cream gravy—luckily, she made a ton of that—and for her part Cat did heat up some tortillas she'd made the other day and opened up a can of green beans.

Neil made the salad, complaining all the while that he was violating the terms of their Sunday cooking agreement, but in truth, it was so he could stay in the conversational mix.

By the time Wesley and Kale got in from church, Neil and Tina were getting along famously. They shot smart-assed comments to each other about their kitchen chops. Everyone was careful where he or she stepped. Barry, letting out his usual croupy mew, could smell the food, but had trouble negotiating the forest of legs.

Neil went to call the boys from their room, where they had gone to change out of their church clothes. Cat chopped up some of the cooked chicken and, scooping up Barry, took him out to the sunroom, with Tina following along.

"He's a beautiful cat," Tina said, watching him nibble on the food.

"Thanks. We used to have to keep him in for Halloween—black cats, you know—but mainly to protect the kids, not him. He was quite the street fighter, gave as good as he got, but these days, he's happy being close to home."

Kale and Wesley inhaled dinner, going back for seconds and thirds, and would have licked the gravy boat clean if Cat had allowed them. After eating, they went outside to shoot hoops in the driveway.

According to Wesley, his JV practices were going well. As usual, whenever his parents asked, he added few details without prodding, but before he went outside, he did mention the coach saying he might be a starter when the season began.

Cat and Neil cleared away the pans and dishes as he kept up a patter about items in the day's newspapers. Things were falling apart in East Germany, he said, but Cat had never been one to pay attention to what was going on in the news. She preferred other places, other times.

Bless him, but if she kept Tina there a minute longer, Cat was sure he would wear her out completely, so after hugs all around, Cat took Tina back to her apartment.

After getting undressed, they collapsed into bed. Cat understood why Tina couldn't sleep last night. She remembered how awkward she felt in the early weeks with Neil, unable to relax around a relative stranger.

She decided not to make any romantic moves, nor rattle on about the artwork or some such time filler. Instead, Cat held her, until after a while, Tina's breathing deepened, her body relaxed, and she drifted off to sleep.

Cat's mind raced as she wondered what to do.

One night together, just one night, and already she couldn't imagine her life without Tina. If someone came across her at the library, they'd see the dry, intellectual crust, and never notice the warmth and fragility underneath.

She thought of how utterly exposed Sherron had looked that day in the supermarket. Cat knew she herself could take whatever people threw at her, and she would move mountains for Wesley's sake, but what could she do to protect Tina, who had the most to lose?

Closing her eyes, she pushed away those thoughts. She listened to her lover sleep, feeling skin against her skin. Cat knew she would be there when Tina woke up, and if that made her late for supper, so be it.

Chapter 16

There was a window in the door between the snack bar and the hospital foyer. It allowed Mandy to watch Sherron through the glass walls of the business office.

She looked her usual self-contained self, but most of the photographs were gone from the desk, except for those containing only her parents, brothers, and/or Emily. Sherron wasn't the type to cut out Ryan, then reframe the photographs. That would be too tacky.

As for her coworkers, one of them changed desks with Marquetta Benson weeks ago to put her farther away from the known homosexual, and the others weren't any better. They talked to Sherron as little as possible.

Mandy wished Chris Delgado, one of the lab techs, would be as standoffish. He wanted Mandy to hear how everyone in town knew she had been caught in bed with Sherron. How hard this must be on Mandy, and did she have any juicy details about her ordeal? Mandy didn't feel like correcting the rumor. No one would believe her, anyway.

Two days ago, Doak Bering warned Sherron that Ryan had hired a detective with a camera to stake out her apartment at night, so no more visits from Mandy; no more contacts at all.

Her father, who Sherron said sounded outraged, believed her home phone might be tapped, which seemed unlikely to Mandy. Sherron didn't want to take any chances. So much for fears of just being caught cohabiting. According to Marquetta, there were spies in the business office reporting back to Ryan anything that could be used against Sherron.

Mandy didn't think Marta would fire her over being involved in the situation, but Marta had her own boss to answer to. As she gazed at Sherron, Mandy thought a sensible person would stand back and wait to see what happens. There was a real likelihood the rumor mill could take them both down. Unlike Sherron, Mandy didn't have reliable relatives.

Besides, she could be as supportive as humanly possible and still end up getting dumped by Sherron for having too much trash in her tree. Come to think of it, though, had Sherron ever made Mandy's background an issue? Sherron liked nice things and, to be honest, was real set in her ways on table manners, but money marked one of the few subjects she'd never been pushy about with Mandy.

"Hang in there." LaSonda Kindred's brassy voice boomed from behind, causing Mandy to jump a few feet in the air.

"I'm hanging."

She peered up at LaSonda, who had a double-clutch of Twinkies in one massive paw, a Dr. Pepper in the other.

"You need to get a message to Sherron?" LaSonda glanced through the window then turned back to Mandy. "I'll go in, raise a fuss about my pay stub, then we'll step out to the foyer. That gives us time to talk."

"Sherron doesn't handle pay stubs."

"Oh, like that matters. Everybody knows I start shit anytime, anywhere."

LaSonda did possess verbal fists of fury. "I got five more minutes before I have to get back, so whaddya want?"

If she intended to back away, this would be the time. Mandy stared through the glass then back at LaSonda, who frowned impatiently. Sherron could use a friend right now. Sherron needed her.

Where was a spot they could meet, someplace a man with a camera wouldn't think suspicious? Mandy remembered Sherron complaining about her hair the other day.

Neil's Better Cuts stood right next to Gabriel Magneto, and tucked behind the folks' shop was a place for Mandy to park. Didn't Cat's band practice in the back of the salon?

They could meet there, that is, if Sherron wanted to. Sherron could make the appointment, then Mandy could follow up to "confirm" the time. Blurting out the details, Mandy waited for LaSonda's response.

"That'll do. You get back to work. I'll find you later."

Back in the lab, Marta Horton was continuing to tweak the new analyzer, which still wasn't working properly.

"There you are," she said crossly.

"Sorry my break took too long. I'll stay late."

Marta threw the manual down on a nearby counter and glanced up at the clock.

"You think you're the only person who's ever done that here? Some days get so hairy, I'm surprised to see anyone come back from break, let alone remember to bring back those pipettes I asked for from Central Supply."

"Crap. Sorry, I'll go do that right now."

Marta grabbed her by the arm as she turned for the door. "Whoa, Nellie. I just had a visit from an ambulatory asshole named Allen Inkston, don't excuse my French. What with our families being members of the same congregation, he said I shouldn't let you near his poor ancient mother.

"Imagine him telling me to fire you when, half the time, you're the only one besides me who can find a vein on Sadie. Did you do what I said about looking into getting registered for spring? Hospital pays tuition and books like I told you already, so get on a stick about it. And where the hell are my pipettes?"

* * *

"Comfortable, are you?" Mary asked.

Tina was soaking in the sun at a table behind the large-print section. She felt such a chill in her bones. It had been a pleasant enough October thus far, but this afternoon, not at all, which made her wonder if tomorrow's drive up to Amarillo would be similarly cold.

"It is nice back here, isn't it, Tina. I thought you'd like to know, the tamale lady's here."

Nesta came around with tamales to local businesses. Why she hadn't also cornered the market in breakfast burritos, Tina could not comprehend. The burrito women had been waging a price war for years, and it's true that Nesta's wares did come a bit steeper than those of Erlinda Aldaiz. Since Nesta happened to be Otilia's sister-in-law, the library tended to be an Erlinda-free zone.

Coming through the stacks, Tina heard Nesta and Otilia having a rapid-fire conversation as Nesta handed over aluminum-wrapped bundles of *masa* heaven to patrons and staff.

Tina managed to pull out some recognizable words. Rico, Ricky, *las putas*—whores, probably an unkind remark about Tantona girls—and several references to *jotas*, which Tina guessed referred to both the local and San Antonio girls, unlikely to all be lesbians.

Tina stored most of the tamales she purchased in the kitchenette fridge then ate a few while standing by the sink. For the first one, it took her a while to organize her fingers to handle stripping off the shuck. The second one, she dropped in the sink, but the next two were easier to manage. She wished she had a little dish of salsa to go with them, not to mention guacamole. She downed four of them and still felt hungry, but enough already.

Tina sat back down at her desk and began working on a book order. Mary came in, giving her a now familiar look of concern.

"You feeling okay?"

"I just needed some food to warm me up. I'm talking to you now. I'm perfectly coherent. Have my clothes on and everything."

Mary pulled the door shut behind her and sat on the corner of the desk.

"Kid, I watched you back there for a good five minutes. I don't know where you were at, but you weren't at that table. I said your name several times; you never looked up. And you haven't been your usual self for a while now."

"I've been dealing with… people, you know."

"Sydney gave you the run-around, and now it looks like to me you're seeing Cat Acuff, since she's been by every day this week. Smart gal. Tough, too. She can handle anything you might throw at her."

At the moment, Tina preferred the old system where Mary pretended not to know Tina was gay, and Tina pretended not to know that Mary knew. Did Tina have absolutely no ability to disguise her emotions? Evidently not, because her friend's face turned even more somber.

"I'm not going to the doctor, Mary. There's nothing they can do for the problem, and I might not have it anyway. I just haven't been sleeping well."

That could be blamed on Cat's lightning raid late last night. A visit she appreciated even now, and that was another reason why her family history had to stay that—history.

* * *

It took on average five minutes to get from the salon to the house. Cat made it in three minutes flat. She rushed through the back door over to the sunroom, where Wesley was sitting on the floor.

Barry was lying in his arms. Her son looked up at her, his face full of dread.

"He's not moving, he's not moving. Do something," he pleaded, refusing to let go.

She lifted Barry's furry head, looked at his face, then felt his shrunken chest for signs of life, but she already knew, and so did her son.

She said to Wesley quietly, "Baby, he's gone." They both started crying.

After a while, she got up to find tissues, then returned. Wesley dried his eyes and hesitantly lifted Barry onto her lap. They stroked his fur together.

"Do you remember how huge he used to be? Y'all would run all over the backyard together. You refused to believe he was a cat, because dogs were bigger than cats. Everybody should know that, even your silly mom."

"He didn't act like a cat." Wesley defended his old position. "I taught him to roll over, and he loved Fritos."

"Yes, he did. He was no ordinary individual."

For the funeral, Neil rescheduled an appointment so he could come home. Wesley, refusing his mother's help, dug a grave over by the west fence. They agreed that it was a good place, for it was near the pecan tree, where Barry spent much of his time hunting birds.

They each took turns shoveling dirt. At the end, Wesley said a short prayer, to which Neil and Cat added amens. After that, there was little time to grieve. Neil had an appointment, Wesley was expected at Kale's birthday party, and for her part, Cat anticipated Tina dropping by to firm up plans for the trip tomorrow to Amarillo.

She would be riding with the family Acuff, and this time, Wesley would be coming along to catch the first set. Mama and Dad then would be taking him back to their house, that is, if Dad didn't explode from the indignity of seeing his daughter in a trashy juke joint, or some other typical overreaction.

Barry in his prime was a good broken-field tackler, a reliable footwarmer, and Wesley's favorite confidante. How unexpected to her that so small a creature could leave so large a hole in their lives.

Chapter 17

Mandy was about to knock on the back door of the salon again when suddenly she stood face-to-face with Sherron. She pulled Mandy in, slammed the door, and started a kiss that went to the piano bench and traveled who knows where else, as neither of them paid attention to musical obstructions.

They were back on the bench, well entangled—how did Sherron manage to unbutton Mandy's blouse without her noticing—and neither was inclined to break apart anytime soon.

Mandy thought the time right for a dose of levelheaded thinking.

"Look, I know what Emily means to you, and this—you and me—this is taking away your concentration. It's going to be a tough fight, and you need all the strength you can muster to get through this thing." Mandy tried to sound confident.

Sherron caressed her hair tenderly. "You want to leave, it'll be on your dime, not mine. Even Daddy knows now it doesn't matter anymore if you're with me. Ryan's out to win. If it weren't you, he'd pay some floozy to jump into a picture with me. I'll take Daddy's advice on us lying low, but only for a little while."

"Why don't you out that woman, the first one, the one Ryan doesn't want people to know about. Why not use her?"

"Ryan doesn't think I have the nerve to do it, because he knows it could backfire on me something bad. Opening motions are in two weeks. He doesn't let up by then, I've told Daddy that Judge Souther's going to hear it all. I haven't seen my baby legally in months, and with that detective on my heels, I can't go sneaking anymore. This keeps up, Emmy's going to start thinking I really don't love her."

Sherron left through the salon. Mandy waited a bit, then went out the back door. She walked up the alley to behind the magneto shop. Mandy discovered her brother, Douglas, sitting on the hood of her white Escort.

Douglas was a little taller than Mandy and more than a bourbon belly heavier. He never took to Mandy, even before they both suspected she might be gay. Back in grade school, he'd beat her up on the playground if she didn't fight back against bullies hard enough to meet with his satisfaction. Douglas graded according to pass-fail and almost always chose the latter.

"I want to know why you didn't front Jimmy the money to help me pay off my speeding tickets." He put out his cigarette on the hood.

"When was that, back in the spring? And now you're asking?"

He slid off to the driver's side and blocked her from the door. "You didn't have the bucks then, I can understand that. But now you're screwing some champagne dyke, and that ain't right. You're not thinking straight."

He chortled over that brilliant stroke of humor. Douglas, at any moment, might give her a punch in the arm or kick in the leg, trademarks of his brotherly affection. Last time he aimed a boot at her leg, she got in a punch before he dropped her. That also marked the last occasion he and Mandy were together under the folks' roof.

"Bet you're wondering how I know."

"Not really."

"I know all, I see all. And I heard Daddy talking to Jimmy about it. Preacher wants Daddy to get with you about changing your sinful ways, but Daddy told them ain't nothing can be done. You're on the highway to hell, you and Bon Scott."

Daddy said nothing could be done, which sounded like an accurate quote. Whatever's going to happen is going to happen anyway, so don't get involved. Unlike Daddy, Douglas gave a damn, even if it was only in the way a boxer cares about his punching bag.

"It's none of your business what I do," Mandy said.

"Then why are you hiding back here, huh? You're next door getting fancied up by that faggot, and we're all supposed to not notice how, once again, you're treating us like shit. Momma's been crying 'cause people won't talk to her at church."

"A lot of those women never talked to her anyway. The folks were better off going to Full Gospel Holiness. That's more their kind of people."

"Do I care? I ask myself. Do I even care what you think? No, I don't. If Chuck was here instead of gallivanting around in Alaska, he'd make you do right."

Despite his words, he took a step away from the car, enough to allow her passage.

"Chuck wouldn't give a rip."

With her attention momentarily on unlocking the door, she failed to anticipate his signature move, the head slap. The whole left side of her head stinging, she forced herself into neutral gear. He wanted an excuse to do more damage.

"Do you want us to fight right now? I have a little time." She drained her voice of emotion.

Douglas looked like he expected more of a reaction. "I'm busy," he blustered, pointing at the shop behind him. "They don't want to see you, so don't even think of going inside."

"I wasn't planning on it."

Safely inside her car, she started the engine then rolled down the window.

"Douglas." He turned around. She gifted him in the face with a half-full Sonic cup and peeled out of the alley. Head slap, my ass.

* * *

Tina sat in the sunroom with Cat, listening to her talk about Barry. Both of them were misty-eyed, Tina more because of Cat's reaction, since she hadn't been around him much.

Tough gal, Mary called Cat. Tough gal possessed a soft spot when it came to pets. Cat had shown her Barry's grave and talked about having a friend create a small, stone marker.

They worked out final details on tomorrow's trip then moved on to the more interesting topic of kissing, but Tina's attention wandered. She worried that her tiredness was showing, that something about her would seem off to Cat.

Back home, she studied the refrigerator and couldn't think of anything to fix. Tamales were easy to handle. She heard Becca's usual decisive rap on the back door. She offered to share, but Becca pulled over a chair instead and handed her a Tecate.

Becca took a swallow from her own can, then came to the point. "What do you think of Gracie?"

"I like her. Do you want to move her in next door? I'm okay with that."

"We're not dating yet. We've been hanging out together, but—oh dear." The realization hit her. "It looks like dating, doesn't it?"

"Most people would call it that. She's nice, and you know you'd be getting free haircuts."

"I know that's right. She said Neil offered her a stall, so she's thinking of moving back, but I don't know. She left me once before."

"Y'all used to be a couple?"

Becca explained that back in the early '70s, she had returned to Tantona to become its first female Hispanic teacher. She spent Saturday nights at a gay bar in Lubbock, where she became reacquainted with Gracie, a former Tantona classmate.

"Then both of you would have known Jack." Of course she would remember her classmate, not that Tina had ever allowed her brother as a subject of conversation with Becca.

"Jack and I went out a couple of times." Becca eyed Tina as though negotiating delicate territory.

"I don't remember that."

"It wasn't for long. I think we were both looking for cover back then. Anyhow, I was at the bar one night when I saw Barbara Wolfe—"

"Cover? What do you mean?"

Becca's mouth made a silent O.

"You didn't know? It wasn't common knowledge. The only reason I knew was because when Jack and I went to the drive-in, I told him why I couldn't, you know, do what everybody else was doing in their back seats that night. That's when he told me he had a crush on Tommy Williams. I don't know if they ever got together."

It was so long ago. Tina could barely remember what Jack looked like before the history hit him. Did he have sex with Tommy? Tina hoped he had, or with Marquetta Benson, the girl he dated back then. Maybe her brother experienced some pleasures in life before he died.

Becca sat there with a patient expression.

"Okay, so you saw Barbara Wolfe?"

"She was with Gracie, but they had a huge argument, and Gracie ended up inviting me back to her house. Anyhow, we fell into being a couple, spent a year or two together, then she left me to move in with some nurse in Lubbock. Gracie can't say no, or couldn't back then, but my friends in Lubbock say she's really changed over the years. But also, there's someone else I've been talking to. She's really deep in the closet. It's too soon to say anything but—are you okay?"

Tina was straightening a picture frame on the wall. It came to her that Becca had been talking for a while.

"Of course. Are you sure you don't want some tamales?"

"Positive. Mom keeps my freezer full. But you go right ahead."

* * *

"I'm guessing you gave Sherron the quickest trim in her life then booted her into the rehearsal room." Cat slowly peeled the crust off her grilled cheese and jelly sandwich. She wasn't particularly hungry. Since Neil viewed her plate as part of his territory anyway, she pushed it over.

"Quick is not the word for it. She's coming in for a manicure next week, so I think I'll finish her cut then. It looks fine to most people, I suppose, but I know what needs to be done. I forgot to tell you, I'm hiring Gracie. She had a lot of clients when she was here before. I'm betting most of them will return."

"I imagine you're right."

"Luis really likes the job in Lubbock." Neil fit his words around an enormous bite of sandwich. His lover had already unloaded two houses in south Lubbock, both of which had been on the market for a long time.

"And you're sure he'll be at the show tomorrow."

"He's driving up. Caterina, you'll love him."

"I'm sure I will." Neil's photographs of Luis showed an Adonis in a full mustache, looking older than twenty-six, but still... It was stupid, but she felt as though she were being thrown over for a younger man.

"We've been talking—I've been talking, that is—about opening up a salon in Lubbock. Luis knows a place that's available. The owner died of AIDS, and his partner can't make the taxes, so we could get it at a really good price."

Neil's voice was starting to pitch upward, a sure sign of anxiety.

"You're moving? What about here? What about Wesley?"

"I'm not moving. I'm broadening our horizons. Luis has a nice bit of money saved up, and I thought, heck, we could swing it from our end. What I'd do is work in Lubbock a couple days a week, that's all. The rest of the week, I'd be here. We'll have a good crew of people here, what with Gracie coming back to town—"

"Do you love him?" she asked, studying his face.

This is what it comes down to. How deep does this go for him?

Neil studied his plate for a long moment, then looked at her gravely.

"Yes."

Chapter 18

"You didn't know I'm gay?" Becca's Tecate appeared in serious danger of spilling from her moving her arms around.

Tommy and Syd were guests at a Tantona Country Club soiree, and Sherron was on Ryan-enforced lockdown, so Hilario and Mandy decided to host a pity party.

Guests included Erlinda, her new friend, Erma Delgado, who was no longer bartending at the Kings Pub, and Becca and Gracie, who appeared to be a couple these days.

Mandy smirked at her housemate, who, caught in the middle of whipping up a *crema*, chopped green chilies, and asadero hot dip, mock-staggered around the kitchen upon seeing Becca.

"*Claro que si*. You were married to Mickey, who's an asshole, but a straight asshole. I mean, *orale, mi reina*, welcome to gay world."

He returned his attention to the contents of the skillet, sprinkling it with various spices. For the party, Hilario broke his no-stove rule.

Gracie gave him a severe look. "Uh-uh, *mijito*. I'm *la jota jefa aqui*."

"More English, please." Mandy had kept up to this point, but wanted to keep Gracie from going full-tilt Spanish. "And besides, the boss of dykedom in this town is Barbara Wolfe."

"That you know of, *reinita*."

"Excuse me, I'm the little queen," said Hilario. "And get me a bowl, it is so ready."

They were gathered around the kitchen table, and even Erlinda appeared to be in a good mood. Mandy thought of how a few months ago, she hardly knew of any gay people in town, and now she knew a roomful. If only she could get one particular lesbian in the room.

"Why don't we call up Barbara? She'd get a kick out of seeing her old house," Gracie said.

Not that lesbian. "She wouldn't come here. She doesn't like me."

"What makes you say that?" Becca appeared puzzled. "Barbara said at the party she thought you and Sherron make a pretty couple. She's not as mean as you think."

Hilario and Mandy shrugged at each other as Grace ran off to use the phone.

His face brightened. "So, is Mickey Reyes gay?"

"No, but he hates women, so he dates lesbians who turn him down, which makes it okay to pay for hookers," Erma said snippily.

That was the longest sentence Mandy had ever heard from her mouth. Erma just outed herself, meaning that Hilario had been right all along.

"Do you think Tommy and Syd might make it here later tonight?" Becca asked.

"You kidding?" Erlinda said. She sprinkled more salt on the dip and gave it a stir. "Come to this neighborhood? They're marrying up, not down. Besides, Tommy's having a trailer installed on his property for Hillie to live in. They'll have their own parties—not that we'll be invited."

Mandy looked at Hilario sharply. That was the first she'd heard about it.

"I won't go until after the wedding—"

"Which is in two weeks." Erlinda broke in.

"Syd wanted it moved up. It's not Tommy's fault." Hilario had a guilty expression.

"And you're gonna be their cook," Erlinda continued, implacable. "You'll be in his trailer, and on his payroll. Then next spring, you'll start managing the *restaurante* for the Anglos. Yeah, you'll be the top in bed and the bottom everywhere else."

Gracie came back into the kitchen. "Darlene said they couldn't make it. Barbara has a cold, but she said to keep them in mind for next time. What happened?"

"It's not even your recipe." Hilario threw the words into Erlinda's face.

This, Mandy suspected, constituted a severe insult.

"She kept buying brisket plates from Jackie's Place until she figured out the recipe."

"You're wrong, Hillie," Erlinda said gruffly. "I wanted to copy Jackie, but I still don't know what all she puts in it. I made so much barbecue that I came up with my own recipe. You go right now, get a plate from Jackie, then get my sauce out of your fridge. You'll see

I'm right. Should Jackie be the one getting help from the Anglos? She's not that Stubbs barbecue man in Lubbock. They know she sells weed on the side. You and me, we're just *jotos*. We'll work for those people. We won't cause trouble."

She turned back to the dip. "I brought some tequila, and I know I saw some limes in the fridge. Let's have a good time."

* * *

The Chopped Club in Amarillo had recently changed its biker clientele to a more mainstream rock crowd.

Tina couldn't tell any difference based on the amount of leather on display, and given how hot the owners kept the place, anyone wearing cow skin tonight had to be sweltering.

Tina had already stripped off her jacket and the pullover sweater. She wished she'd worn a lighter tee. It was only near the end of Blue Movie's first set. The night could only get hotter. She had a spell of drifting off during the ride up to Amarillo, but didn't think anyone in the car noticed, except perhaps Cat. At the moment, she felt somewhat together, but who knew how long that would last?

She was sitting with the Talamantez family. They were a large group to try to figure out who's who, so Tina didn't. Next to her sat Luis, Neil's sweet but quiet boyfriend. Cat's father had such a look of loathing on his face whenever he looked at the two of them that Tina felt they must have the word "Homo" branded on their foreheads.

Earlier, the route from the Talamantez home to the restaurant had taken them by Tal's Auto Sales—a large, showroom house and a large, showroom business—which reinforced her impression that Cat had been raised a blue-collar princess.

Juan Talamantez pointed out during the meal that Cat had been expected to transition into the white-collar world as did her brother, a dentist. Cat served as National Honor Society president her senior year and would have graduated top five, if not for a certain problem.

The so-called problem, Wesley, was there at the table eating a giant rib eye and to the relief of many, not paying attention to the conversation. Tina thought the man rude. His attitude hadn't improved.

"You want to dance?" Luis asked. She would do anything to get away from that glowering face across the table.

Luis took advantage of the slow pace of the power ballad to bring Tina into his arms. He yelled into her ear, "So, are you as in love with Cat's father as I am?"

"Even more," she hollered back. "I feel like such a diesel dyke around the man."

"Oh, he's not a homophobe. He just hates queers, that's all."

They dissolved into laughter, prompting frowns from the other dancers. They probably thought "If You Don't Know Me By Now" did not need a Weird Al makeover.

Wesley seemed to be having a good time hanging near the bandstand with a female cousin. All through the evening, Tina's internal monitor kept track of her behavior. She felt acutely aware that her public role was as best friend, not lover, which meant no lingering touches; no touches, period.

Wesley accepted Tina as Cat's friend, the library lady, so what was Juan's issue? Maybe he acted this rude toward all of Cat and Neil's friends. She wanted to be supportive of Cat, but there was no way she wanted to be around that man again.

* * *

It had been an infuriating, exhausting evening thus far, during which Cat did manage to spend a little time with Luis after the first set.

He was a smallish, sweet soul who looked younger than his photograph. Maybe he came off differently during the day, dressed in a suit and more in need of a shave, but in dim light, he looked like a boy wearing a fake mustache.

Cat felt the moment needed captions, as in a foreign movie:

Cat: "It's so great we get to meet. I've heard so many good things about you."

Caption: "Don't take my son's father away. Borrow him, but don't keep him."

Luis: "I love your music."

Caption: "Aren't you kind of old for this sort of thing?"

That morning, she had gone over the numbers with Neil. She agreed with him on the need to expand into Lubbock and perhaps beyond, given that neither of them wanted to be sweeping up hair cuttings when they were senior citizens.

It didn't sit well with her that the idea had been prompted by his wanting to be closer to his lover, but now, after meeting Luis, who could blame Neil?

She kissed Wesley goodbye before Mama hauled him away to the car, and then she walked back toward the table alongside the dance floor. She intended visiting with Tina before end of break, but Dad blocked her path.

Cat was reminded as she looked at him of how her father always preferred to be described as Spanish, this despite his Valley accent and a skin shade worthy of a sun-beaten Apache.

Success was what mattered to him, not what he abandoned along the way. Her getting pregnant, opting out of college, and marrying a hairdresser—her failures were many, but the biggest one was her refusal to believe he was always right. From that, all sins flowed.

"Let me have it."

Dad unpursed his lips to speak. "Caterina, I have heard you sing worse."

From him, that registered as praise. Why did he find it so hard to dole out a compliment? Even tonight, which already should count as a triumph—Mama, her brother and her cousins, every single one of them gave the band a standing ovation—even tonight, Dad retained his ability to reduce her spirit to ashes. The band should never have come to Amarillo. She should never have allowed Dad to poison this night for her.

She wanted to tell him to go to hell. She settled for her usual role as the set-up stooge for an insult comic.

"What do you think of Tina?"

"Who? That woman? She doesn't dress proper for a librarian."

"She's not going to be checking out books in a bar."

"I know what's going on," he said fiercely.

"You have no idea—"

"I saw the look in your eyes when she said something during the meal. You think you're hiding it, but I saw it. You're the man, aren't you? I don't have to ask. That's what you are to her. This is what comes from your marriage to someone who cannot satisfy you. You go looking for women. And now you bring one of them to us, and what are we to do, eh? There is no blessing to give, not from us. And there also is your boy to consider."

"My problem, you called him."

"Only for that time, that time only. Wesley is growing fast, and you cannot be seen as having relations with that thing."

"Tina, her name is Tina. I would rather die than hurt my son, but until Tina—"

Why was she bothering? He rarely allowed her to finish a sentence, much less let her equal him in an argument, so what would change tonight? Nothing, but she would have her say, regardless.

"Until I met her, I had never truly been kissed before." Cat's voice wobbled despite her effort at self-control.

"It's such a small thing, I know. I had no idea what opening myself up really meant, or how deep my emotions could go. She's an amazing woman, Dad, not some 'thing' to scrape off your shoe. I'd thought about her for ages, but until recently, I didn't have the guts to do anything. I'm not afraid anymore, and as for receiving your blessing, you've never given me the time of day. I don't expect anything from you.

"And, about Wesley? One day, Dad, he'll come to me saying he's in love with a girl. Love, Dad. That's not an academic subject to me anymore. I'll know how to talk to him about it, because I'll have experienced it in my own life. I'll know."

Dad looked upset, yet strangely enough, he was letting her speak. She had to finish.

"I have no idea how it's going to play out with Tina. All I know is that I've finally joined the human race."

She walked over to Tina, who was chatting by the bandstand with Luis and Neil. Cat took her by the arm and gave her a light kiss on the cheek, knowing that Wesley, currently cooling his heels in her parents' Cadillac, was not a part of the viewing audience.

"Are you okay?" Tina asked, surprised.

Her family and her band were all looking at her, waiting to see what would happen next. Barflies and dancers perched around the floor waiting for some sign of life.

Cat stood motionless.

"You're feeling like you're the show," Tina said.

Cat managed to nod her head.

"You're wrong. We are looking at you, but it's what comes out of you that matters. What you sing and what we feel when you sing, they're not the same thing. What I get out of your music isn't what Neil gets. And what you feel when you're up there, no one knows except you.

"All you have to do tonight is sing and not get in the way. We'll take care of the rest."

Chapter 19

"I'm telling you, the numbers are going to be way down on the next census." Sadie Inkston's visitor, to judge from his weathered neckline, ought to be at the Tantona Café drinking coffee with the other retired farmers rather than holding down an uncomfortable chair in a patient's room.

Still, it ranked as a charitable act, paying visits to the sick, even if Old Farmer had yet to speak a word in the patient's direction. All his attention appeared focused on the younger Mrs. Inkston, who had about as much interest in the topic as Mandy did.

She checked through her slips again while she waited for the nurse's aides to finish changing the sheets. It was another simple stick on this nice old lady who had been socked in Room 102 for the past several weeks. Deathwatch, she guessed, but Sadie wasn't cooperating. Good for her.

Mandy idly examined Halloween decorations on the hallway opposite her. She was trapped for the moment listening to Old Farmer.

"My boy told me the school's going down a class next year, and since the Chaco patch is running out, there goes the oil revenues—town's going straight to ruin—don't you agree?" He directed the last comment toward Mandy. "Paper gal, right?"

"I used to be."

Mrs. Inkston appeared offended that the lesbian was being acknowledged in her mother-in-law's room, so Mandy decided to stretch out her reply.

"You're right, Chaco is running out, but they're drilling by the Post highway down near the turn to Brookeland. That's supposed to pay out big time."

"Young folks leaving, though." Old Farmer had his theme in a death grip. "My grandson is taking a job in Dallas, and Junior would move to Lubbock if he could find a buyer for his acreage."

Mandy searched her mental Rolodex, trying to place the old man's face with a name. She believed that she had seen everyone in the county during her reporting days, many of them more than once.

The aides left, their arms piled high with linens and a soiled pillow.

"It's my little angel," Sadie said to Mandy.

"That's right."

The steps had become routine. It was better if she didn't think at all during the stick. Just give the spot a go with an alcohol wipe, feel a likely vein underneath the skin, then slide in the needle and fill the tube. She found the vein. Time to stick and fill.

"Did you get it?" asked the younger Mrs. Inkston.

"Yes, ma'am."

Pressing down on the spot with a cotton ball, Mandy waited before she laid a strip of tape over it. Chris Delgado didn't take enough time with the old folks, who tended to be on blood thinners and didn't need much excuse to bleed anyhow.

Mrs. Inkston was ticked that Mandy hadn't left yet. She grabbed the ice pitcher and went off to the nurse's station, loudly grumbling about the quality of help these days.

Steinhall. Old Farmer was Colin Steinhall, who owned pretty much the south end of the county. Would Ryan be the grandson about to move to Dallas?

"There're plenty of anesthetist jobs in the Dallas area." Mandy chose a nonchalant tone.

"I wouldn't know, but he thinks so. Now, you need to tell the paper man he ought to be writing the truth. I'm tired of all the happy talk and people buying barbecue sauce when the town is falling down around our knees."

Mandy said she agreed foursquare with Mr. Steinhall, then left after giving Sadie a gentle pat on the arm.

It was a hectic Friday morning, and there didn't seem to be any chance for a break. Feeling desperate, she asked Marta if she needed something from Central Supply.

"No." Marta's head was bowed over a microscope.

"Are you sure?"

Mandy knew she was pushing it, but what else could she do, since the hearing in Sherron's case was scheduled for Monday. Sherron and her lawyer could complain all they wanted, but if Emily was shipped off to Dallas over the weekend, then Judge Souther, a Steinhall crony, would see it as a done deal. Sherron would be stuck with making long drives to Dallas for her court-supervised visits.

Marta gave Mandy her usual lightning blast. "Take that bucket of used needles out to the incinerator—turn it on—get me a diet Coke."

Mandy grabbed the container, fled down the hall and out the back door by Central Supply. Tossing the container into the incinerator, she flipped the switch, then ran back inside, taking a sharp turn into Central Supply. The clerk there took her smoke breaks seriously. Good, the desk was empty.

Marquetta Benson answered her phone with the usual canned greeting. Mandy forced herself not to interrupt. Marquetta had to sound normal to the spies in the office. Moments later, she strolled into Central Supply. Marquetta had been priceless to both Mandy and Sherron in arranging meetings and digging out information on Ryan.

"What's this about?"

Mandy told her what she had learned.

"That son of a bitch." Marquetta looked chagrined at either her choice of words or the volume, or both. "I already set up an operation at the library this afternoon, but this puts a new spin on things."

"Operation?"

"Let's just say my daughter Lauren has become Emily's new best friend. That's suspicious right there, because Emily's the student council type and Lauren, bless her heart, is a total jock, but we've been relaying messages between the girls all week trying to set it up."

She shook her head. "And now Ryan, that jerk. I hadn't heard a word about him leaving, but I did hear that he was taking some vacation days next week. Figured it was because of the case, but now we know. I'll slip Sherron a note in a folder. We've worked out a little system. Okay, I gotta run."

"Thank you. You've been really nice through all this."

"Sherron never looked down on me like a lot of people did when Lauren was born." Marquetta was about to expand on that when the Central Supply clerk came back from her smoke break.

Marquetta jumped into a conversation that sounded well in progress about some supply problem involving paper for the business office, then led Mandy out the door.

Without another word, Marquetta, who should have been recruited for military intelligence, glided down the back hallway route toward her office, while Mandy bolted for the snack bar to buy Marta's Coke.

She snuck a peek through the glass window at Sherron, who was about to find out how bad a day she was having.

* * *

Each morning there was a blind wakening, a fumbling breakfast, then the earth snapped into orbit, and Tina was fine for the walk to work.

Mornings were turning cooler as October began running out of days. Soon, walking would become problematic on several levels. But if she switched to driving, she'd have to decide if she could negotiate the eight-block route home after work. It was later in the day that things got shaky.

By mid-afternoons, she couldn't find the thread anymore. She stared at book catalogues until something or someone, usually Mary, broke the trance. It seemed like a Coke helped, and two Cokes were the perfect eye-opener, but then she felt jittery until late evening, when a strange confusion would come over her.

Then, only a couple of Benadryl shut her down enough to sleep, and she had to sleep if she didn't want to find herself stumbling through the house again.

She thought she was eating enough, but she was losing weight anyhow, just like Mom did. Mom would pile her food high, toy with her portions, and then end up dumping the entire plate in the trash. She couldn't remember how Jack ate before he got really bad, only that they worked so hard to get food down him.

Mom never talked about her family, but Dad, who grew up in the same Central Texas neighborhood as her family, got around to sharing the history with Tina one afternoon while they were sitting in Jack's hospital room.

Mother's oldest brother died of Huntington's, as did her father and an uncle, and probably more members than that, but the history had a way of breaking up families.

Some of them stayed to take care of the sick, but others moved to places where no one knew about their traitor blood. For a few family members, the illness created violent twists before they ended up in wheelchairs, ended up in graves.

That created a powerful motivation for her parents to move to the South Plains. It was an excuse not to tell their children about the history. Make a family, then see who survives. The gamble failed.

Tina never had children, even though when she was a young teen she loved babysitting and looked forward to becoming a mother. She had locked down her life, piled high her savings, because she knew what might happen.

She knew these foggy afternoons might come.

She rationalized those closet encounters with Sherron, but then she reached out to Syd, then to Mandy, and at the end, to Cat. Call it doubt, or hope. Doubt, because for many months the fog and restlessness had been sporadic, attributable to stress. Hope, because why not hope?

She didn't know, not for certain, and the not knowing made a little space for someone like Cat. Now Tina had to close off that space, starting this week with turning down visits at home and work, and the past three nights, not returning phone calls.

It had to be done, even though she couldn't stand hearing the hurt in Cat's voice. Cat already knew the history, but she wasn't in too deep, Tina hoped. Cat could step away now and not feel guilty, Tina hoped, for Cat's sake.

Today she had to be especially sharp, so she had been sipping on Cokes all afternoon. Tina heard the rumbling sound of George Bering's deluxe van, what he called his chili wagon, pull up in the back parking lot.

She closed the front door of her office and waited by the back entrance. George unhurriedly opened the sliding door of the van to disgorge Sherron, who took the time to straighten out her dress and collect her purse. George then pulled into a parking spot, keeping the motor running. He loved the element of intrigue.

The Steinhalls' legal maneuverings had prompted Dale Lawrence, a friend of George, to take an interest in Sherron's case. That could only be for the good.

Although the rumor mill had the man in the midst of his own marital problems, he was a well-connected local lawyer. Marquetta said on the phone he advised Sherron that, while the library stealth visit technically stood in violation of the court order, what "ol' Souther don't know can't hurt him, which means that twit is damned near Superman."

Slipping into the kitchenette across the hall, Sherron sat down in one of the two folding chairs Mary had set out earlier. Her face seemed well composed, but her hands would not keep still.

"Would you like a drink?" Tina offered.

Sherron was about to answer when the knock came. Tina creaked her door open a notch and answered irritably, "Yes?"

Mary Eckert had Lauren, Marquetta, and Emily standing behind her.

For the benefit of Otilia and any other staff, volunteers, patrons, and passing cars in the vicinity, Mary boomed, "I know you don't like to let loose of books until you're good and ready, but I have two girls needing to see a reference book for a report they're writing."

"I'm trying to finish up a report of my own. They can come in, but they'll have to read it in here. I don't want to lose track of it."

The girls and Marquetta then scooted inside, and Tina closed the door. She knew Mary would find reasons to remain close by in case Otilia decided to barge in without knocking, which she was prone to do.

Standing in the kitchenette doorway, Sherron reached out for Emily who rushed into her arms, both of them weeping, both of them trying to speak. Emily was a solemn, brown-haired girl with her mother's cheekbones, and seemed likely to inherit her father's height, as she was already eye-to-eye with Sherron.

Tina sat back down at her desk and tried not to watch. Taking her cue, Marquetta took Lauren over to the end of Tina's desk to look at a reference book Tina had pulled. In order to boost their cover story, Tina had already made copies of a section Marquetta said pertained to an actual school assignment.

Tina glanced over and saw Sherron and Emily huddled together on their chairs. Sherron was stroking her daughter's hand and talking quietly.

"But, Mom," Emily burst out at one point, "it's not right."

Tina turned her head as though from the scene of a car accident. She thought of how she once despised Sherron. She didn't anymore, and she was thankful that she didn't have children, for Emily's pain, while acute, was temporary.

Even if Ryan got his way, eventually Emily would turn eighteen and couldn't be stopped from seeing her normal, healthy mother. Who would want a child to see end-stage Huntington's?

"Hey, how's it going?" Marquetta said with forced cheer. She gave Tina the look.

"Were you dating Jack when he started getting sick?" Tina wished she could unspeak her words.

Marquetta had just risked her job and helped a friend violate a court order, yet Tina had the nerve to ask her about something that happened decades ago. The smile vanished from Marquetta's face. She glanced at Lauren, who was a near-perfect mirror of her mother.

"He dumped me," Marquetta said. "After that time he went walking out of class and ended up over by the football field, he dumped me. At first, I wondered if it might be because people didn't like him dating someone who's not whiter than white, but Jack didn't care about things like that. I didn't know what was going on. He didn't come to school anymore, and then my parents told me about the illness.

"By then, I was going out with another boy. I did go visit, but you probably don't remember, because there were a lot of kids who went to see him at first. I'm sorry." She added the last words with an agonized expression.

"I'm sorry I asked. That was a long time ago."

"He was a sweet boy. It was terrible what happened to him. So unfair."

Worried, Lauren took her mother's hand, but then there came a knock on the back door. It was George Bering, the chili man. Sherron and Emily would have to say goodbye to one another.

Sherron applied tissue to her daughter's face, carefully blotting away any evidence of tears.

"Now," she said with a deliberate calm, "you're going to walk out there without a care in the world. I love you, no matter what, and Daddy, even though we don't agree right now, he loves you, too. I will see you again, so don't fret about it, and, no, you're not running away. I won't have it. No daughter of mine is going to go tromping down some dirty old highway. I will get this thing worked out. Count on it."

* * *

Cat could hear Gracie's radio through the rehearsal room door blaring out some god-awful Milli Vanilli tune. It was probably giving Sandra a stroke, but as advertised, Gracie hadn't had an empty chair all week, and she drew numerous male customers.

Still wearing a stunned expression, Neil sat on the piano bench next to Cat.

"You're sure you didn't know?" she asked. "You don't remember Tina with her mother at the nursing home? Nobody's ever mentioned the story to you, you're certain of that?"

"Caterina, you're the lesbian, not me. I usually don't pay much attention to attractive women. I can't imagine why you'd still want to see her. Doesn't that thing take, like, years, and they die, anyway? You'd be stuck taking care of her, when this is the time you should be finding someone with, I don't know, more long-term prospects, and don't forget Wesley."

"Oh, the way you're remembering him right now, coming up with a scheme to spend time in Lubbock instead of with your son?"

An unfair remark, but her temper was boiling over.

"I am thinking of him. I'm not going to move my male lover into our house. People would talk."

"Why not? Put Luis in the guest bedroom and make him pay rent. Tell Wesley any story you want, even the truth. It's not as though your parents visit much anyway. Mama would be fine with it, and I sure as hell don't care what Dad thinks. No one can come in and steal our child the way Ryan's doing to Sherron. We're safe. As long as y'all aren't going after it on the kitchen table, I don't see the problem."

Neil moved over by the drums to put a little distance between them. They had never come close to blows, and their arguments were rare, but truth be told, Cat's volume during a spat could drown out a 747 at takeoff.

"I don't want Wesley to get hurt."

"What hurts him more, lies or the truth? I think you're the one who's afraid. You're afraid he'll hate you for bringing your lover around, but he won't. You never know, he might turn into a smart-aleck, but having gay parents will be the least of his problems by then. Wanting to meet girls, and figuring out his goals in life, that's what he'll care about."

"Bullies, what about bullies?" The strain showed on Neil's face.

"I know what you went through at Brookeland, getting beat up 'n all, but Wesley's different. He's straight, for one thing. He's popular at school, and from the way the coach talks, they may end up moving him to varsity by the time district rolls around. Jocks automatically get a free ride in life. He can handle it."

She dialed down the volume and tried to sound more reasonable than she felt.

"Tina's not talking to me, but I'm going by her place tonight, and we'll have it out. I know what's going on, she knows I know, and I'll be damned if she gets all noble on me."

Besides, she added silently, there's a good chance I'll chicken out if I don't do something fast. Here I'm giving Neil a pep talk about courage, and I'm the one about to crater.

Chapter 20

"This is truly a bad, bad idea." Mandy knew better than to expect Sherron to agree, and she didn't.

"I'm ending it. My baby's torn into pieces over this. If the judge takes her away from me, he takes her away, but I'm going down guns blazing." Sherron aimed for perfect alignment in the parking place.

It had already been such a crazy, jumbled day, what with Hilario moving out, Gracie moving in, boxes everywhere in the house, then a madhouse at work. Now she was Sherron's captive for a visit to Dale Lawrence's law office at five-thirty on a Friday evening. Dressed in jeans and a tee, Mandy neither looked nor felt prepared for legal doings.

"Let me stay out here. It would just set Ryan off."

"That's the idea. I need him off balance." Sherron handed over an envelope. "Hang on to this. I dashed over to the bank at lunch to get this out of my safety deposit box. I thought I'd need it Monday. I need it now."

Petrified, Mandy trailed Sherron into the office. Her family didn't mess with lawyers except for reducing sentences, that sort of thing, and Daddy, for one, had never been able to afford Dale Lawrence.

She saw a serene face at the secretary's desk. It was Darlene, Barbara Wolfe's girlfriend, who nodded as Sherron paraded past. Okay, Mandy thought. Let me carry the train, because although I am totally irrelevant to this situation, I'm here anyway.

Clutching the envelope, she went inside Lawrence's office. It was packed with Ryan and his lawyer, Duke Montgomery, Judge Souther, Judge Walt Burlow, George Bering, and now Sherron and herself.

Dale Lawrence, his glossy white hair combed into an impressive pomp, briskly kicked off the proceedings.

"Co-counsel had a case in Amarillo—deposition—unable to make it, but Mrs. Steinhall agreed that I could provide adequate representation. Am I right?"

He aimed the remark at Sherron, who nodded.

"There's no need to pussy-foot," Dale said. "We know why we're here. Mrs. Steinhall has a letter in her possession that will clarify the court's position regarding her alleged homosexuality. The court will discover that the plaintiff had due knowledge of certain proclivities prior to their marriage. May I have the letter, please?"

Mandy handed him the letter, then eased back into a safe place next to Mr. Bering. He smiled proudly at her as though she had performed open-heart surgery, which it felt like, to be honest.

Ryan, his hair trimmed short, was wearing an expensive gray suit. He gave Mandy an angry look. Okay, Sherron, you got your wish, Mandy thought. Will I escape this room alive?

"Since the plaintiff has demonstrated intent to remove Mrs. Steinhall's daughter to another locale, this is indicative of his reluctance to come to terms with Mrs. Steinhall in this matter. Therefore, it is incumbent upon me as Mrs. Steinhall's representative—"

"Just show 'em the letter, Dale," George said.

Dale glared at him, then opened up the envelope and drew out a letter. "This is the only copy. And only the people in this room have prior or current knowledge of this copy."

At that, he paused, and kept pausing. Darlene opened the door.

"Dale," she began, but then Roberta Burlow, Judge Walt's wife, walked through the door. Ryan looked crushed upon seeing his aunt, but Roberta had an air of defiance in her erect bearing.

"There's no need to read through my letter, boys. My husband knows all about it. We worked through the problem years ago."

Judge Walt's wife and Sherron. Sherron couldn't have been older than eighteen, since the affair took place before her wedding. Roberta had to be at least twenty years older. She was well preserved, with touches of gray in her dark brown hair but still, robbing the cradle. Bitch.

She felt Mr. Bering's arm on her shoulder, reminding her to remain calm. Ryan wasn't the only one in the room with a desire to go to war.

Judge Walt didn't appear as calm as his wife. He may have known about the affair, but he didn't look thrilled to have it brought up in a divorce action.

Duke Montgomery stepped forward. "We ask that the letter be stricken from the record."

"Oh, good gravy, Duke, we're not in court, so quit the lawyering talk," Roberta said. "Ryan, don't be a jerk about this. You knew the deal going in, and so did Sherron. Marriage didn't take with her. It did with me, except for moments of weakness that my husband already knows about.

"I don't want my kids and grandkids to hear about this, so I'm putting all of you on notice. This better not end up on the grapevine. As for you, Ryan, you work things out on custody, or that little story you told me about Maria Munoz's surgery? That might end up with their lawyer."

Ryan's face turned ashen. He gulped in some air, then pulled Duke with him into Dale's restroom.

Shortly, they popped back out. "I believe we can come to an agreement mutually satisfactory to all sides," Duke said. Ryan made little effort to hide his distress.

It didn't take long after that. Roberta and Judge Walt left with the letter, followed by George Bering.

The lawyers hashed out the custody agreement and divorce settlement in under thirty minutes. Court papers would be filed Monday morning. Ryan agreed to turn down the Dallas position, and Sherron could spend Sunday afternoon with Emily in her apartment without supervision. Sherron would have every other weekend with her daughter, as well as alternate holidays and one month in the summer.

Even with the letter and Ryan's cave-in, Judge Souther was disinclined to grant unrestricted joint custody. Maybe Sherron had pushed the ball down the field as far as she could go.

Darlene stopped them as they came by her desk. "I thought y'all would like to know. Barbara just called me. She heard that Tina's in the Emergency Room."

"What happened?" Mandy knew a possible explanation.

"I don't know. LaSonda had the ward clerk call. Barbara said somebody found her lying unconscious on Shelton Street. Ambulance brought her in."

"Dang it," Sherron said. "She shouldn't have been trying to cross Shelton. Fool-headed drivers don't pay attention. Let's go."

As they ran to Sherron's car, Mandy repeated the 23rd Psalm over and over. Tina had been living in the valley of the shadow of death for a long time. If ever anyone needed still waters and a healing touch, it was Tina.

"Don't worry, sugar," Sherron said. "The Lord is taking care of her right now. I have every confidence."

* * *

First came a brilliant light then fuzzy shapes in the perimeter. She felt a twinge in her ankle, as well as an immovable stitch in her right side and a stinging sensation in the crook of her left arm. She wasn't in the afterlife, then.

Even if God's hell existed, Tina figured the pain would be a lot less selective. She seemed to be thinking coherently. Focus, come on, focus.

She saw LaSonda connecting a small bag to a larger bag on her IV. "Good, you're back. Stay with me a little longer this time. What's the last thing you remember?"

She vaguely remembered walking out the back door of the library. "Not much."

"What's today?"

That she knew. Tina answered a series of questions and tolerated LaSonda's pushiness on shining an even brighter light in her eyes. LaSonda gave way to Dr. Schaust, a skinny, wire-haired terrier of a man, rumored to be a drug abuser.

"Aren't you the lucky one, getting me on call? Another fifteen minutes and I'm turning you over to the resident. He should be in by then. I imagine he'll recheck your neuros. In the meantime, I'll take a crack at it."

After repeating many of LaSonda's questions and adding some more, Dr. Schaust stood back from the table to allow the lab tech to draw blood.

"Where's Mandy?"

"She's not on tonight," the tech said. "I drew your blood when you first came in. You don't remember?"

She did something crazy, of course, like walking into traffic. This would be the first of many hospital visits for her, so while she was still able to be cooperative, she needed to make a good impression.

Complimenting the tech on his skills, Tina was surprised when Dr. Schaust started talking about admitting her to the hospital.

"Why? There's no treatment for it."

Dr. Schaust did a double take. "Excuse me? It may not be my specialty, but I've seen a lot of cases, tons of them. I figure, two or three days to get you regulated, a nutritional consult, and you'll be good to go. You're in pretty good shape, considering you haven't been under a doctor's care—which I think bears repeating. You haven't been under a doctor's care. Now you are. There is most definitely a treatment for what you have, and once we get you straightened out, we might be able to fix it with diet alone."

She was missing something. Upbeat didn't surprise her, but this man acted supremely confident.

* * *

Becca brought Cat a cup of coffee from the nurse's station. They were holding vigil in the waiting room across from the emergency room.

"My cousin works evenings, and she said you don't want to try the snack bar coffee. It's nasty." Becca stirred more sugar into her own cup.

"Thanks for calling me."

Cat had heard the siren down the street, seen the ambulance speed by, and thought nothing of it, because she was so wrapped up in working out a new client's tax mess, and figuring out how to approach Tina. Well, Tina would be very approachable right now, if not for the immovable object of LaSonda, who did allow that there was a possibility of a visit once Dr. Schaust finished.

Gracie came through the entrance, closely followed by Neil.

"I called Hilario just as soon as I heard," she said, teary-eyed. "Oh, the poor woman. He told me of her problem, and I pray to God that they can find a cure."

First off, you barely know Tina, Cat thought fiercely, and let's not remind Neil that I waited a while to tell him about Tina's health issue.

Neil gave Cat a reassuring hug. They went down the hallway for a little privacy. He cleared his throat nervously.

"Look, I've been thinking about it. It's not my place to tell you who to fall in love with. I put my cards on Mimi, but damned if she didn't turn straight on me. As for Tina, whatever you want to do is fine with me. We'll deal with it, okay?"

Dr. Schaust came into the hallway at roughly the same time Mandy and Sherron shot through the entrance

"Are you the Ransom family?"

"Yes." The group spoke simultaneously, then Becca continued alone. "All she has is a father who lives downstate. I'm going to call him as soon as you give me a report."

"Then let me give you a report. She has no broken bones, but there are some deep contusions from her falling down."

"She didn't get run over?" Gracie asked, breathless.

"No, the driver stopped in time. Ms. Ransom is a very lucky woman, as she could have gone into a coma at any time, even died in her sleep. Collapsing where she did meant she received immediate care."

Dr. Schaust remarked, "It's the first time I've ever heard someone laugh when they get the diagnosis. After all, it's no longer an automatic death sentence, but most people aren't thrilled when you tell them they have diabetes."

"Pardon?" Cat said. "She has Huntington's Disease."

"Not today. At the moment, she is your basic, garden-variety diabetic, and if she hadn't been putting off seeing the doctor—hello? I'm open for business—we could have been taking care of it already. As for Huntington's, I saw no sign of it."

Suddenly, Mary and Barlow Eckert, George Bering, and Otilia Garcia hurtled into the now-jammed hallway.

"I suppose you're all related to Ms. Ransom," Dr. Schaust said dryly.

"Of course we are." Otilia delivered an extra helping of bile.

"She just has diabetes," Becca called out to the newcomers.

"Isn't that great news." Barlow Eckert got a word in before the general hosannas.

Chapter 21

"So, how many gays are there in Tantona?" Mandy helped Hilario move the last of his boxes into the back of his pickup.

"We'll never know, will we?" He plopped down on the tailgate and beckoned her to join him.

Tommy and Syd's wedding was scheduled for three o'clock at Tantona Country Club. Hilario said he had plenty of time to finish moving into the trailer before driving to Lubbock to meet Syd and Tommy after their wedding. The three of them would make a lightning trip to Las Vegas, after which everybody was due back at work Tuesday.

It didn't sound like a romantic honeymoon to Mandy, but it'd be hard to apply the words romantic or honeymoon to such a cold-eyed marital transaction. Maybe Hilario would have some quality time alone with Tommy while Syd shopped or played the casinos.

"I hope it works out for you."

"Tommy and me, we'll be together, or as together as we can make it. You know, Syd was so freaked when she heard about Tina last night."

"I thought she was way over Tina."

"You don't know Syd like I do. She's never over anything, but at least she has someone new." His voice trailed off.

"Who?"

"I'm taking the lady to Lubbock with me. I can't tell."

"Of course."

It would be another spy, she figured, someone Tantonans would never peg as being one of *those* people. Good luck. Hope you fail. Equally true emotions.

Sherron pulled up just as Hilario's truck rounded the corner at a fast clip. She stepped out of her Town Car carrying an overnight bag. Mandy opened the front door and let her in, knowing too well that Sherron was not one to put up with femme niceties. Sherron could carry her own bag, thank you very much.

"Would you like something to drink?"

"Yes, please." Sherron placed her bag by the sofa then followed Mandy into the kitchen. "It has been such a morning. I went by the hospital to visit with Tina. She's doing much better. She and Cat both said to tell you hi."

If Mandy hadn't been such a coward, the two of them may never have gotten together. Now, Tina had to deal with a different crippling disease. It said something about Huntington's that diabetes would seem like a cakewalk by comparison.

"Thank goodness," Sherron said, "I always go on a cleaning binge when I'm stressed out, because otherwise I'd be down on my knees right now scrubbing the kitchen floor in my house. It's already spotless. You know, I want everything absolutely perfect for my baby girl."

Sherron took a sip and gave Mandy's kitchen a speculative look.

"You're not cleaning anything here."

"Fine." Sherron pretended to be in a huff. "Do you think you can come over tomorrow, say, around two?" she said in a more mellow tone. "Just for a little while, so you and Emily can get acquainted. There'll be cake."

"Sure. What's with the bag?"

"I thought that since it's okay now for you to sleep over some nights, I thought, well, I could do the same here. If that's all right with you." Sherron actually looked unsure of herself.

"I think it'd be okay. In fact, we might do a little cohabiting right now." Mandy drew Sherron into her arms. She got to make the first move for a change.

* * *

Maybe she bounced a few times when she hit the ground, or a truck did run over her, because Tina felt sore all along her right side. She couldn't complain about the fall, as it saved her life.

Cat put down the diabetes handbook that the hospital had provided. She was sitting on the side of the bed.

"This is okay, I guess, but I'm sure you have books in the library with a lot more information."

"I do, not that I've ever read them, unfortunately."

"Oh, and do you read everything you buy? Tell me how to rebuild an engine, then, or how to fly a kite," Becca jibed from her chair by the window.

Tina felt amazingly clearheaded, despite her bumps and bruises, as though the sunlight coming through the blinds possessed restorative properties. A goofy thought, she realized, but these days, that didn't mean a personal apocalypse.

In her phone call to Dad earlier, she made sure she sounded well on the way to recovery, trying to take any pressure off him to visit.

Ruby, who was listening on another line, was having none of it. "We're driving up today. You're in for it now, young lady."

What did it hurt if her father came up to see her for a change, instead of Tina always having to make the trip down to Houston? He hated Tantona, said it brought back too many bad memories. Tina allowed herself the next thought. *Dad, it's okay to come up now. I won't die on you while you're here.*

"What are you thinking?" Cat asked.

"That I'm lucky to have you and to have such good friends."

"You know it." Becca glanced at the door, her expression changing to disbelief.

There in the doorway stood Syd, in full makeup and a yellow silk dress. There was a flower in her hair, and her eyes bore their usual level of alarm.

"Syd," Becca said, "aren't you supposed to be doing the meal thing right now, getting ready for the wedding?"

"I told Tommy I'd be right back. How nice to see you, Becca."

"It's good to see you, too," Becca answered, with the same odd degree of formality.

"I just wanted to come by and check on you," Syd said to Tina. She didn't move from the doorway.

"We're taking good care of her, so don't you worry about it." Cat stood up and cocked her head at their visitor.

Okay, Tina thought. Girlfriend's being very protective right now, although Syd doesn't seem hostile the way she did at Mary Eckert's party.

"Have they said when you'll be discharged?" Syd gave Cat an apprehensive look.

"Monday, perhaps. It depends on the blood work. I hope the wedding goes, that it goes the way you want it to." Tina had no idea what the appropriate thing to say might be. Emily Post likely didn't have a chapter on closeted gay weddings.

"It'll be great. Tommy and I, it's what we've been wanting, both of us, and his family has been very supportive."

"I can imagine," Cat said curtly.

"Okay, I need to get back to it. I just wanted to say hi." Syd hastily began her withdrawal.

"Let me walk you out." Becca hustled to catch up with her.

Tina smiled at Cat. "So, are you always going to be that subtle around my ex-girlfriends?"

"Only her, and just this once, to make a point."

"The point being?"

"That she can't ever raise a hand to you again, or I'll turn her into a lefty."

"Whew. Aren't you the pacifist? And did you catch the byplay between Becca and Syd?"

"I'm afraid so. That can't possibly work out."

"You think Syd coming here, that that was her last hurrah before going even deeper in the closet?"

Taking Tina's hand, Cat looked at her solemnly. "I was sitting in the salon just two blocks away, and there you were in the middle of traffic doing your damnedest to die or get killed, either one."

"I'll do anything to get attention."

Cat leaned over and kissed her. She took care to avoid the scrape on the right side of Tina's face.

"I love you," Tina said. She thought, no, don't be pushy. This can't be the right time or the right place, not after being together for such a short time.

"I love you, too," Cat replied. "You need to know I was getting scared about your symptoms. I told Neil yesterday I was going over to your apartment to confront you, but then you ended up here. I'm saying I might have ended up talking myself out of being with you."

"The Huntington's, it could still happen."

"I don't care. Just don't freeze me out. Please don't ever do that to me again."

They were holding hands when Neil and Luis came in to pick Cat up for lunch. Neil gave Tina an affectionate peck on the forehead.

"You're looking quite delectable."

"Don't lie to the girl." Luis came around to the other side of the bed to plant his own kiss. "Institutional white is not her best color, but we'll take care of that soon enough."

"What do you mean?" Cat asked. Her husband and Luis both looked so conspiratorial.

"I went looking at houses this morning." Luis managed a few words before Neil jumped in.

"There's a big one on the Lubbock highway about ten miles north of town, the Baker place. You know, the guy who got sent down for tax evasion."

Luis took over. "And his ex-wife wants to unload it. For a song."

"A song and two choruses," Neil said. "From there, Lubbock's twenty-five miles, which is an easy commute."

"What's this about?" Cat asked.

Luis gave her a searching look. "I thought you and Tina, it was like with Neil and me, that you were ready. We're going to need the extra space now. The property has about a zillion square feet. There's even a basketball half-court in the back, which Wesley will love. But, if you're not—"

"How much are we talking?" Cat asked.

"She's asking one-twenty-five, which would be about right in Lubbock, but I think that's overpriced for here," Luis said.

"I have seventy-two-thousand dollars in savings." Tina acted as though she had just quoted a weather report.

"Good Lord, woman. How did you manage that?" Neil was the first to speak, but Cat had pretty much the same reaction.

"When Dad sold the house, I received half the proceeds, which wasn't much, but I've been adding to it ever since. I thought I'd need it to die on. And now, why not live on it?"

"Oh, sweetie, let's do evens. We'll all put in," Neil said.

"Are you sure, Tina? I don't want you to feel pressured." Cat felt almost giddy.

"I feel the total opposite of pressure, for the first time in my life. I don't care what people might say about it. It's what we want to do that counts."

"Neil, let's have an incredible housewarming party, okay?" Cat said. "When the time comes, we'll get Mary Eckert's guest list from her party. We'll have all of them come over."

Tina sat up straighter in the bed. "And Luis, roll up the blinds, would you? I feel like letting in some light. For all of us."

Author Kelly Sinclair   Photo Credit: Amy Spencer

About the Author

Kelly Sinclair lives in Temple, Texas, but is a transplant from the South Plains. She has been a reporter, a rock singer-songwriter, and is currently a librarian. One of her poems appeared in the *Texas Observer* political magazine, and her computer-derived prints are featured in art galleries.

Sinclair has worked with an experimental art-rock ensemble, written country songs for such Texas acts as the Maines Brothers, and sung backup for funk bands and bluegrass performers. In her writing, she follows a similar path of exploring her creative boundaries, writing scripts, plays, and musical song-cycles.

Coming soon from Blue Feather Books:

Lesser Prophets, by Kelly Sinclair

We were the despised, the unloved, the fitfully tolerated, the novelty acts, and in some fortunate places, the embraced and even cherished.

In those safe harbors, we celebrated each stage of our growing emancipation even though others of our tribe were faced with hangman's gallows or less deadly alternatives and dared not show their true faces. We passed as "normal" when possible, and we were penalized when we could not pass. We only had freedom when they said we could be free. That was our world. We knew none other.

But then God, or Fate, or the Omniscient Divine—or merely happenstance—negated all the rules, and our status was forever changed.

This is how the new world began. We were the *Lesser Prophets*, and this is our story.

Detours, by Jane Vollbrecht

It should have been a typical day of trimming shrubbery and edging lawns, but Gretchen VanStantvoordt—known to everyone as "Ellis"—first gets caught in a traffic jam and then lands in the emergency room with a badly sprained ankle. Mary Moss, a newfound friend who was caught in the same traffic jam, convinces Ellis that trying to tend to her dog and negotiate the stairs at her walk-up apartment while she's on crutches isn't such a good idea. Without friends or family in the vicinity, Ellis accepts Mary's offer for assistance.

When Ellis meets Natalie, Mary's nine-year-old daughter, she's ready to make tracks away from Mary as quickly as possible, but her bum ankle makes that impossible. Ellis stays with Mary and Natalie while she recovers. Little by little, Ellis develops a fondness for young Natalie... and develops something much deeper for Mary.

Ellis and Mary work out a plan for building a future—and a family—together. Destiny, it seems, has other plans and throws major roadblocks in their path. Ellis is forced to reconsider everything she thought she knew about where she wanted to go in life, and Mary learns that even with the perfect traveling companion, not all journeys are joyous.

No GPS can help them navigate the new road they're on. Come make the trip with Ellis and Mary as they discover that when life sends you on a detour, the wise traveler finds a way to enjoy the scenery.

From Hell to Breakfast, by Joan Opyr

Wilhelmina "Bil" Hardy is at loose ends—and in the small college-town of Cowslip, Idaho, that's a mighty short length of rope.

After a long struggle with non-Hodgkin's lymphoma, and an even longer struggle with the law, Bil's brother Sam has died. Bil is devastated, but she has no time grieve. Her sisters, Sarah and Naomi, seem to be dating the same cowboy, but neither knows they're sharing. Her girlfriend Sylvie is having mother troubles. Her role model, lesbian separatist and commune-builder Captain Schwartz, is having ex-husband troubles. And, worst of all, Bil's parents have sold the family home and bought 200 acres on a remote hillside from a notoriously crooked businessman. Bil's mother, Emma, is looking forward to evicting local drug dealer and Sam's erstwhile pot supplier, Jake the Snake, from a run-down shack on the hillside, but someone beats her to it—with a shotgun.

Who killed Jake? What's the unwelcome news from Captain Schwartz's ex-husband? Who is pushy preacher George Knox and what does he want? And, most puzzling of all, what do Bil's sisters see in bow-legged two-timer Buck DeWitt? Bil must answer all of these questions and more while trying to keep her relationship with Sylvie from going AWOL. Holy Cowslip! It's business as unusual for Bil and her crazy Idaho cadre.

Coming soon, only from

Bluefeatherbooks
LIMITED

Make sure to check out these other exciting Blue Feather Books titles:

Tempus Fugit	Mavis Applewater	978-0-9794120-0-4
Yesterday Once More	Karen Badger	978-0-9794120-3-5
Addison Black and the Eye of Bastet	M.J. Walker	978-0-9794120-2-8
The Thirty-Ninth Victim	Arleen Williams	978-0-9794120-4-2
Merker's Outpost	I. Christie	978-0-9794120-1-1
Whispering Pines	Mavis Applewater	978-0-9794120-6-6
Greek Shadows	Welsh and West	978-0-9794120-8-0
The Fifth Stage	Margaret Helms	0-9770318-7-X
Journeys	Anne Azel	978-0-9794120-9-7

www.bluefeatherbooks.com

Printed in the United States
218827BV00001B/9/P